"Strong prose, gritty characters that jump off the page, and a fast–paced plot join forces to make this an exciting series!"– Katie (K.E.) Ganshert, award–winning author of *The Gifting* series

Great characters and an engaging plot with several twists will keep readers glued to the pages. Definitely a series to grab for fans of cold–case detective stories who will enjoy a sci–fi twist. – Tressa, Wishful Endings

I'm not telling you how to live your life, but don't miss this series. Just don't. You can thank me later. – Courtney

I couldn't be more excited to see how this unforgettable series wraps up. – Kelly

Every single time I meet up with Rembrandt Stone, I know I'm in for a twisting and wild ride. – Suzie

This whole series deserves so much more than five stars. I have NEVER been as hooked on a series as I am on The True Lies of Rembrandt Stone. – Beth

I'm on the edge of my seat with a roller coaster ride of emotions waiting on the next book. Seriously, just when you think it can't get better, Rembrandt Stone takes on a whole new life that will keep you begging for more. – Necee

I love this series and I feel like the stakes are raised with each book in this series. The suspense is there, the moments that pull the heartstrings and moments of humor that perfectly balance all the intense moments. It is the perfect balance of all things I love. – Nicole

The action is heart pounding as we move with Rem to right the wrongs of the past so his future can be whole again. Trust me the pace kept going and I'm now very anxious for the final part. Excellent series and I never read time travel fiction… – Shona

The authors have blown me away once again by surprising me at every turn. There hasn't been a moment when I've ever felt I knew what to expect. The only thing I know is that anything can happen. – Mimi

THE TRUE LIES
OF REMBRANDT STONE

CAST THE FIRST STONE

NO UNTURNED STONE

STICKS AND STONE

SET IN STONE

BLOOD FROM A STONE

HEART OF STONE

HEART OF STONE

TriStone Media Group
Minneapolis, MN

Tristone Media Inc.

15100 Mckenzie Blvd

Minnetonka, Minnesota, 55345

Copyright © 2021 by Tristone Media

ISBN: 978-1-954023-10-9

www.RembrandtStone.com

SOLI DEO GLORIA

CHAPTER 1

They say that without hope, people perish.

I say hope crushes the soul.

That's why I look away when Frankie Dale's beautiful gray eyes fall on me as I walk into Alexander Malakov's third-story office.

The pulse of some electro-dance beat pumps in from the nightclub below, the odor of bodies and a hint of reefer saucing the air. Turbo is on fire tonight, the line to get into the club a half-block long despite the sultry July-heated evening.

Alexander leans against the front of his desk, his arms folded over his gray silk Brioni dress shirt, his cuffs rolled up—as if he'd actually do any of the bare knuckle work it takes to keep his multi-million dollar organized crime empire running.

That's why Vita, Alexander's "XO," the guy who delivers his orders, called me. Vita is shorter than me, lean, blond and about my age, his face heavy with lines and a scar that runs from his eye to his chin.

We're work friends.

"Staz," he says in greeting and I nod at him and walk over to Alexander. The female—she can't be Frankie, not right now—sits on the sofa. I can't tell if she's been roughed up, but I don't look at her, just in case.

"Thanks for coming," Alexander says from his perch on the desk.

"Of course, boss." I've played the undercover game for years, so this can't be any different. Booker briefed me earlier—wait for that, I'll catch you up—and apparently, I've been at this game for years, so sliding into my persona as Staz, Malakov's right hand thug is an old shoe.

According to my sketchy research, Alexander Malakov runs the biggest Russian gang in Minneapolis, filling the void after Burke and I took down Somali warlord Hassan Abdilhali some twenty years ago. According to Booker, Malakov's also recently declared war on the police department, hoping to carve out his own Little Moscow in the North Loop.

I remember this part from past versions of my life—my 1994 Porsche 911 having recently been a victim of this war.

And I know you're wondering—past versions?

Again, wait for it. It's worth it, I promise.

Alexander is vaping, and now sets down his cigarette. My guess is that it's filled with high end snow because he's edgy and ticking with energy. I walk over and put a hand on his shoulder. "You okay?"

"How did she get in here?" He directs the question to Vita, and I look at him, expecting an answer, too.

"I don't know. We found her in here rummaging around. Say's she was lost, but I don't buy it." Vita says.

Now I look at Frankie.

The sight of her makes me pinch the corners of my mouth and take a breath. Her lip is bleeding, although that could be from a struggle. Frankie has it in her to cause trouble, thanks to her parentage.

I know for a fact that Booker doesn't know what she's up to. But then again, she's in her mid-twenties and can make her own decisions.

If she were my daughter, I'd put a tracker on her.

Okay, not really, but the thought catches me, and I inhale sharply.

I *had* a daughter. Once upon a happier time. With blonde hair and blue eyes and the kind of laughter that made me believe in things like hope, and faith, and love.

For the last month, I've tried to believe—to hope—that I could find her, save her, bring her home. I haven't succeeded.

Remember what I said about hope?

Alexander brings me back to point when he says, "Staz, I want to know how she got in here." He looks at Frankie. "Make her tell us." He then looks back at me. "And then get rid of her."

Frankie makes a sound, just a small one, from the sofa, and I wonder if it's for show. But when I look at her, and she lifts her gaze to me, a real tear drips down her cheek.

I wonder if she knows me, this smart, vibrant, nosy daughter of my mentor.

Probably not. Because, according to her father, I've been playing this undercover game for many, many years.

To the world, I am Staz Kalenin, head of security for Alexander Malakov, head of the Brotherhood in Minneapolis.

My head still pounds where I took a hit last night in a fight down at Quincy's—and it wasn't a spar—where two bros go a couple rounds in the ring—but a real fight, with thin gloves and blood and the sound of breaking bones.

I won, but it hurt.

"Do we really want the heat of a dead body right now?" I say to Alexander, as I gesture to her with a head bob. "She doesn't look like trouble."

Okay, she does. She's dressed in a leather bustier, a pair of black shorts and five-inch heels. Booker's head would explode if he saw her.

And I wonder, suddenly, where Zeke is. When I last left them, in our previous lifetime, Frankie and he were dating.

Ah. The light shines upon my pounding, webbed brain. Zeke had the code to Alexander's office.

I have no doubt Frankie lifted it from him, somehow.

"She's trouble, all right," Vita says and walks over to her. I think I save both Frankie's and my life when I don't move as Vita grabs her dark hair and yanks her head back. He leans over her. "Maybe, after you talk to her, you give her back to me."

I know the Brotherhood traffics women, and I'm not sure he doesn't mean to sell her.

Yeah, that isn't happening. But I lift a shoulder. "We'll see."

Her gaze darts to me and for the first time I narrow my eyes at her, something that says, *I got this.*

She glares at me, so maybe she didn't quite pick that up. Then she plants her heel in Vita's ankle.

He shouts and I cross the room and grab his wrist as he reels back to slap her. "Get out," I say.

Vita is in charge of operations, so technically, I don't answer to him.

I think.

Vita jerks away and looks at Alexander. He too has gotten up, picking up his e-cigarette. He nods to Vita, who informs me of his current emotional state with a word, then they both leave the room.

The door closes, and suddenly we're alone.

I have a gut feeling Vita is standing right outside the door.

She looks up at me, and tears course down her cheeks. But her eyes are bright, as she says, "I know you won't hurt me."

Really? Because remember what I said about hope? And you saw Vita...

One of us is probably going to die.

CHAPTER 2

4 hours earlier

I hurt everywhere. Not just because I'm soaked through, the rain outside having found my bones and turned everything achy and raw. And not just because I've recently gotten my bell rung in a brawl, one that flared to life an old shoulder wound. And especially not because I've just returned to a world where my beloved remodeled craftsman home doesn't belong to me (but to my brother-in-law Asher) where I've murdered my best friend, and where I live the life of a gang thug, but because...

My wife Eve is dead.

And has been for twenty-three years.

And, worst of all, I can't change any of it.

"Tell me again what happened to the watch?" I'm staring at a cup of coffee—my third—and outside, the world is black, rain pinging against the tall windows of a late-night eatery appropriately titled, the Hard Times Cafe, located off Riverside Avenue, downtown.

It's not full this time of night, but not deserted either, the night club crowd trickling in. We're seated at a table, a neon blue coffee sign reminding me of my deficits, and I hold up my half-empty cup to a passing waitress while I try to focus on John Booker's words.

John Booker. Who is back from the dead, alive in this timeline to help me sort out this nightmare.

He's changed. Less hair, and it's mostly white now under a gimme cap from the Minnesota Blue Ox hockey team, his dark brown eyes still alert, still wise. He's in his late seventies, by my calculation, and the years are etched on his face, in the white grizzle that layers his chin. He's wearing jeans and a faded blue shirt, rolled up above the elbows, and most of his clothes are soggy.

After all, it took a bit of cajoling to get me out of the rain-soaked graveyard where I was camped out at Eve's tombstone hoping—maybe even praying—I might wake up.

Hope is a mocker.

Booker is scrutinizing me, probably looking for the changes inside me that will prove I'm not the man he knows in this lifetime.

"It stopped working," he says now, in answer to my question about the watch. "Twenty-three years ago, to the date." He leans in, cuts his voice low, and I know why.

Despite the late-night crowd—many of whom are probably already tanked—he doesn't want anyone to overhear the truth.

We are time-travelers. John Booker and I, in two different eras, via the same magical watch. He passed it down to me after his death, the purpose of which was to go back and solve my cold cases.

I might have used it for other reasons. Like to stop crimes. And sleuth out a serial killer who arose after my first circle back into time. And recently, to take said serial killer out of the picture before he could get started and eventually kill my daughter. And my wife.

So, admittedly, not the intended use, but in theory, thematically the same.

I did stop crime.

Apparently, Time or Fate or whomever is at the helm of this project doesn't agree.

"What do you mean, *stopped working?*"

"I mean, I can't travel," Booker says. "My cold cases are still cold." He's wearing the watch and now shows it to me, as if I can somehow detect the minuscule changes that have occurred to strand us in our own time.

The watch is old—with a fraying leather strap and the kind of open face that shows the gears inside, now frozen. For the record, they're always frozen unless the wearer is traveling back in time. Then, they work for forty-eight hours or until the crime is solved.

I didn't solve the last crime—and maybe that's the problem, and I suggest this theory to Booker. "I was investigating a liquor store shooting, a man named Min-Jin, who owned Jin's Liquors."

"I remember that case." He's staring at me. "You saved my life. And his."

Bingo. And maybe I shouldn't, but I can't help but add, "First time around, you both died."

He sighs. "Rembrandt. You know the rules. You can't change things."

We've been through this, a number of times, actually. "I know. I'm just supposed to get justice for the crime. If it makes you feel any better, you weren't supposed to die in this shooting. You were originally supposed to die years later, from cancer."

He raises an eyebrow. "Which is how you got the watch." Then he smiles, nodding, as if confirming something to himself.

It's a long story, but at the time, I thought Booker was punishing me from beyond the grave for leaving the police force. I had my reasons—most of them were tied to my seven-year-old daughter, Ashley and not leaving her fatherless.

By the look on his face, I see now that he meant the inheritance as an honor.

Huh.

"So you changed something, and left a case unsolved."

"Could that have broken the watch?"

"No," he shakes his head. "I've done that—left a case unsolved. And…changed something. And neither of those times did the watch stop working."

Now I raise an eyebrow because, well, like I said, we've been through this, and every single time it was Booker reading me the riot act. That scoundrel. I should have known he'd already been there, done that.

As if reading my mind, he holds up a hand. "I know, I know. Just… leave it, okay."

I know that look. I give him a nod.

"Anyway, when you leave a case unsolved, it stays unsolved, but the watch still works for the next case. Until…well, it stopped working. What did you do?"

I have no answer for him. And I'd love to know what *he* changed. Deep in my gut, I think it has something to do with me, but now isn't the time.

My only goal is to save Eve. Which means, we have to get the watch working.

He leans back in his chair as the waitress returns to warm my coffee and give Booker a plate of sausage and biscuits smothered in gravy.

I look at it. "How have you lived this long?"

"I stopped smoking. And this—well, my fiancée has me eating green protein shakes every morning." He makes a face. "But one moment of freedom won't kill me."

"Heart disease might," I say, but I'm a hypocrite because the waitress returns with my order of Frito Chili Pie.

But this body can handle it. I'm lean, and tough and I might be hurting, but it's the kind of hurt that says I know how to handle myself.

Still, I'm needing some comfort food after the last two hours.

Truth is, I would still be face down in the mud if it weren't for Booker's words in the dark of night, when he found me, "This isn't over yet."

Please, God, although I'm not sure all of this isn't his fault.

"Fiancée?" I say, picking up on that. "So, you didn't stay married to Frankie's mother?" I ask, referring to the wife he had when we last met, twenty-three years ago.

He frowns. "That's right. You don't know. My wife died about five years ago from cancer."

"Wow, Booker, I'm sorry." But at least Frankie grew up with her father at home. I have a very clear memory of her at six years old, her dark hair in pigtails, waving to me in the police station as her father, the chief, took her to work.

He's not the chief of police anymore, and I wonder if my old partner, Shelby, is at the helm, like before.

"We had eighteen beautiful years together, raised our daughter and were happy. I think that's about all a person can hope for."

I look at him, my throat suddenly raw. "What if I told you that I had that, too, once upon a time."

He's mid bite, and now puts his fork down. "Before the watch."

"Yes. You willed it to me, but I didn't get it until about two years after your death. At the time, I was retired from the force, was trying to re-ignite my writing career with a true-crime novel, and Eve Mulligan and I were married with a beautiful little seven-year-old girl, Ashley."

I've lost my appetite, the words turning to shards in my throat. I can hear my voice cracking. "I went back in time to solve the case of the coffee shop bombings."

"Of course," Booker says, finishing his bite. "Ramses got out of jail about six months ago."

Ramses Vega, the perp. Funny that Booker would know that, but maybe he keeps tabs on his former collars, too.

"Mariana still doesn't believe he acted solo."

"He didn't. He hired someone to make the bombs—a guy named Leo Fitzgerald."

His eyes narrow. "I know that name."

"He was killed twenty-three years ago…by me." The day I turned into a murderer.

"Right," he says, again putting his fork down. "I remember that. You were exonerated—self-defense."

Huh. I hadn't expected that.

He wipes his mouth and raises an eyebrow. "You have something to confess, Rembrandt?"

"He was a serial killer. He murdered thirty-eight women."

He picks up his coffee, leans back in his chair. "I'm listening."

"Something I did the first time I went back in time unleashed a serial killer. When I returned to my time, I discovered that he'd killed twenty-plus women. And…" I place my hands on the table, take a breath. "He'd killed Ashley."

He is quiet, and looks at me without recognition and I realize…

He never knew her.

It's like a punch to my sternum.

"She was my daughter. Seven years old."

Now, he purses his lips, nods. "I'm sorry."

"I went back again to try and figure out what happened, and returned to find Eve married to Burke—"

Again, nothing.

"Eve was my wife, Booker. My *wife*. Ashley's mother."

"Okay."

"It gets worse. Burke was terribly injured in a fire that also killed Danny, so I stopped that—"

He winces, and I realize how far I've veered from the intent of the watch.

"And when I came back, the serial killer had upped his game to thirty-eight women. I narrowed it down to Leo Fitzgerald this time, a man who had eluded the police for twenty-three years, and found him here, in our time, in Florida. But after I arrested him, he broke out of lock-up and killed Eve. Now, in this time. I mean, that timeline, which is this time—whatever, you get it, right?"

I sound like I've been on the sauce and I reach for my cup of coffee.

"I think so," he says. He leans forward again, his coffee on the table, his eyes on it, as if trying to sort my words.

Me too. Because if I hadn't lived it, I wouldn't have believed it either.

"My last circle back was to stop the serial killer. That is the history you know."

He looks at me. I nod. Hold his gaze.

"And?" he finally asks.

"I did." I don't need to go into the details, but in case you missed it, it wasn't entirely on purpose. Things got complicated. Although, admittedly, if I hadn't gone to his house, Leo would still be alive.

I would have thought a court of law would find me guilty of murder, in the second degree, at the very least. I'm not sure how my lawyer conjured up a self-defense plea from what happened. But I can admit I'm glad I'm not in jail.

I do wonder if Eve had something to do with that.

Eve. "I thought I'd return to Eve, alive. And Ashley, alive and…" Here's where I swallow the dusty lump in my throat.

"Instead you find yourself working undercover for Alexander Malakov."

And when he says it, quietly, something akin to a vise releases in my chest. Because, I just wasn't sure.

I have it in me, I think, to be exactly the man I met two hours ago in a darkened alleyway. The man who beat the tar out of a younger man.

I scared myself, a little. But without Eve in my life, what did I expect?

"Where do you want me to start?"

I like the fact that Booker knows what it feels like to reenter your world, mid-stride, having no idea how you got there.

"Eve." Where else?

He runs his thumb over his coffee cup. "She was murdered twenty-three years ago today. At least that's when we found her body."

I push my food away and fold my hands in my lap. I admit it—I'm trying not to shake. "Where? How?"

Because if he's right, then she died while I was still back in time.

"We found her in the trunk of a car, in the middle of the parking lot at Minnehaha Park. She'd been strangled."

I draw in a breath. "Sexually assaulted?"

He shakes his head and I can breathe again, although like I said, everything hurts.

"How did you find her?"

"She called you, and her phone was still on her. We think the killer must have driven her to the location, and then killed her. We traced her call to your phone, then pinged her location."

She called me. I close my eyes because now I remember the missed call. The voice mail I never heard.

I might be ill.

He's quiet for a moment. Then, "You and Shelby found her."

I look at him. And suddenly I'm glad I don't have every memory. "Did the Jackson murderer kill her?"

"Who?"

I inhale. So I *did* kill him. Leo Fitzgerald did not become a serial murderer of thirty-eight women. This should loosen the vise in my chest.

Not even a little. "Then who killed her?"

He shakes his head. "We don't know."

I still and my chest locks up. "She's a cold case?"

His indrawn breath tells me the truth. I lean back. Asher, Eve's brother, told me this before, right after I returned, when I went to our house to find her. He said a lot of things I haven't gotten my head around yet. "You've got to be kidding me."

"I wish I was."

"C'mon—I have to have been on the case—"

"Really? Not on your life, Rem."

I blow out a long breath. "I didn't handle it well."

"How could you?" His eyes are suddenly kind. "You loved her, more than any of us realized, and it tore you apart." He pushes his food away too. "I blame myself. I should have seen how wrecked you were, but you wanted to work—told me you *had* to work. So I let you join Danny's gang-violence task force, with Burke."

Burke. The man I killed. "What happened? Asher said I *murdered* Burke."

21

He meets my eyes. Then, nods. "Murdered isn't the right word. But yes, you killed him."

I just stare at him because… "No. That can't be right, that—"

"It was an accident. You two were investigating a drug-related case, and you'd gone to the suspected headquarters of a local drug dealer. Burke was killed in the crossfire. By you."

He doesn't look at me when he says it, and I frown. "It was an accident."

"Yes."

Silence.

"Okay, Booker, what aren't you telling me?"

He sighs, shakes his head. "It gave you exactly what you wanted to join Malakov's crew."

I'm not connecting the dots here.

"You went to prison for a year. And your cell mate was—"

"Alexander Malakov."

He nods, and I shake my head. "This sounds like something I would have concocted—"

"Yeah, it was your idea. We used Burke's shooting to strip away your police creds, put you in a cell and let you earn his trust. You broke out of jail—"

"Convenient. I'm sure I had help."

"Not that much." He offers a slight smile.

"And then I became what—Malakov's thug?"

"And our inside man. You've spent twenty years feeding us valuable information, stopping human trafficking and slowing the flow of opioid drugs onto the streets."

"While doing Malakov's dirty work."

Booker lifts a shoulder. "You've never crossed any hard lines."

I look away because I well remember my years working undercover in my original life. No, I never crossed any hard lines.

But the gray ones got pretty blurred.

He finishes his coffee. "Recently, the Brotherhood has declared war on the police. Our guess is that they want to drive us out of the North Loop, where Malakov owns a couple night clubs, most of the housing, and has his thumb on the local businesses. He'd like a police-free zone."

"I'll bet," I say. "In my last go-round, he blew up my Porsche in that same war."

"We'd really like to know why Malakov decided to wage war now. What triggered this?"

"Besides a thirst for power?"

"He's been at the helm since his brother went to prison twenty years ago. We know Boris recently got out, so maybe he's the trigger. We need you to find out their plans, and maybe even the catalyst for this. If we know that, maybe we can go to the source and shut this down."

I glance at the watch.

He follows my gaze. "That's not an option. Rem. Let's be honest. You've completely missed the point of this timepiece. You're not supposed to change—"

"Then what good is it? I'm a cop. I'm here to stop crime."

"You're a detective. You *solve* crimes."

"What happened, Booker? What happened in the past?" I meet his eyes. "What did you change that you can't live with?"

He draws in a breath, looks away.

Fine.

"I'm going to figure out how to fix the watch, Chief. And then I'm going to find out who killed my wife and stop it."

He looks back at me and his jaw is tight. "How? Even if you get the watch working, you know how this works. You can't go back to Eve's case—she'll already be dead."

"Then I'll go back to the liquor store murder."

His lips tighten as his chest rises and falls. "You can't repeat a case."

I close my eyes as the truth rings inside me.

It's over, and Eve is dead. And there is nothing I can do to bring her back.

I look at him, my eyes burning. "Why did you tell me this isn't over? You lied to me!"

He holds up his hand, looks at the patrons around us, but I don't care.

Eve is *dead.*

In my pocket, my cell phone rings, and I pull it out.

Vita. I met him earlier tonight, at the fight. Russian, blond hair, a scar dissecting his face from his eye to his jaw, lean and a little bossy.

I think I work for him.

"We have a problem," he says. "At Turbo." He hangs up.

I guess that means I'm being summoned. "Where is Turbo?" I ask Booker.

"It's a downtown club."

I pocket the phone. "Give me the watch." It's not a request.

To my surprise, he takes it off his wrist. I put it on mine and stand up. Hold out my hand.

He stands up, too. "I like this version of you much better, Rembrandt," he says. "The other guy has given up."

I don't blame him.

But not me. Find the glitch. Fix the watch.

Save Eve.

One last time.

CHAPTER 3

I suppose it gets easier to become someone you don't recognize when you walk away from yourself.

I killed Leo Fitzgerald. And something inside me shifted—I felt it then, two days ago, and I see now why I look in the mirrored wall and don't recognize myself.

My eye is swollen from the cheap shot Meelis gave me during our fight, and I wear a few other scars on my face—a gouge out of my jaw, another along my hairline, but that might be from the crowbar a perp named Bryce Mattson beaned me with a couple days and twenty-three years ago.

Despite the clocking he gave me, he was a kid and I wish I could have saved him.

My hair is shorn high and tight, and it makes the planes of my face stand out, all hard, lean angles. And, I'm built—I've put on at least twenty pounds of muscle, mostly in the upper body.

All that thuggery builds muscle.

My clothes have mostly dried, but I still feel grimy, although that might also be from my current situation.

"I want you to find out, Staz, where she got the code. And then

get rid of her."

Oh Frankie, what are you doing here? My mouth tightens at the corners.

"Please don't hurt me," she says quietly.

I feel sick. She doesn't know me. Which tightens my gut because I'd hoped she did.

Hoped she remembered a kinder, gentler me.

One who would never hurt her.

The fact that Alexander gave me this job, however, tells me that man is gone.

I *have* crossed hard lines.

"I'm not going to hurt you," I say quietly. "Just sit there and let me think."

She stares up at me, almost in disbelief, and maybe I don't know what I'm doing, but there's a part of me who believes, despite the image that stares at me in the mirror, that I haven't strayed that far from myself.

When I worked undercover, so many ages ago, I had a lifeline, someone I could call if I got in over my head.

You guessed it—that person was Burke. I had him on speed dial, and I just had to press the number, and he had my back.

I scrub a hand down my face and pull out my phone. I don't know who's on the other end of my speed dial, but I press #9, then drop the phone back into my pocket.

My dark hope—and you know how I feel about hope—is that Shelby is picking up on the other end.

"Frankie, what are you doing here?"

Her mouth opens. "How do you…" Frankie pulls her legs onto the sofa and pushes herself back and away from me. "How do you know my name?"

I pull up a nearby armchair and sit across from her. If Vita looks in the window, it'll look like we're having that prescribed chat. And maybe we are.

"I've known you since you were just a kid," I say. "In fact, I'm the reason your father is still alive."

She swallows.

"Yeah, you'd better be scared because I know you're a grown woman, but when the Chief finds out—"

"You're—"

I hold up my hand, and she closes her mouth. "Listen, if we want to get you out of this, we're going to need some help—*and I hope whoever is on the other end of the line is listening*—and you'll need to buy us some time. So, spill."

Her mouth tightens. She shakes her head.

"Listen. I'm—"

"I hacked it."

I frown. "What? Aren't you a reporter?"

She frowns too, and shakes her head.

Huh.

"What do you mean you *hacked* it?"

"The lock. It's not that hard. I used a fluorescent latent print powder and a UV light, and found the residue from the buttons."

For a second, I feel like I'm listening to Eve, back in the day when we solved crimes together. "Are you…how do you know to do that?"

"C'mon, don't you watch cop shows?"

Never, actually. And, sorry. There's no way I'm going to believe she's a cop. Not under Chief Booker's watch.

Still, her getup tells me this isn't the Frankie I left behind in a previous timeline.

I'm suddenly remembering Zeke's words, right before I left them, in the rain. *"Will we know?"* A quiet pleading to not destroy the life he'd carved out with Frankie.

Sorry, Zeke. I honestly didn't see this coming.

"Okay, we can sort it out later. Right now, we need to get you out of here." I stand up, move the chair away and grab her by the arm. "Play along."

Her eyes widen as I haul her to her feet. "What? How do I know you're not really going to kill me?"

I look at her and I suppose this does need to look real, so, "You don't."

Her mouth opens and I drag her across the room to the door. Open it. She starts to scream, but I pull her against myself and clamp a hand over her mouth. Vita is standing there, like I thought, and he looks at me, a smile cracking his face.

"My turn?" he says.

"You wish," I snap. "I'm taking her downstairs."

He backs away, his mouth open a little and then, "Finally. Or I should say—what is it about this one? You've never—"

"Because I like her," I say, although there's a roil of sickness in my gut, especially the way she's struggling in my arms.

I'm playing the jerk, but a tiny part of me releases a shout of relief. I *knew* there were some lines I wouldn't cross.

Vita is nodding, like he approves of my descent into debauchery, and stands back as I pull a struggling Frankie down the hallway, toward the stairs.

"Stop," I say, growling into her ear. "I won't hurt you."

She slams her heel into my ankle, clearly thrilled with our game. I bite back a grunt and get her down the stairs, and then the next flight, the one that leads into the club.

I have no doubt that every square inch of Turbo is under surveillance—Malakov will see if I just let her go. But maybe, if there's a crowd—

She hits me again with that spike and this time I release my hand over her mouth. The music is raucous, bodies packed onto the dance floor, despite the late hour, and I realize this is the after-hours club.

The one where Greenies, Blow, Crystal Glass, and plain, old-fashioned Dope can be found on the menu, along with the fresh batch of trafficked women and possibly even men.

I understand now how I've survived.

After Eve, I had no soul left to destroy.

We stand in the stairwell, my hand still on her arm, and I know Vita is just upstairs.

It's likely we're on camera.

I lean in close to her, grabbing her around the back of her neck, my mouth against her ear. "Frankie. You have to promise me that, no matter what happens, you'll disappear. Because I'm going to let you go, and they're going to ask me why. And I can't be sure I won't tell them."

I lean back, meet her eyes.

Hers widen. "Rembrandt Stone?" her voice is barely heard above the music.

I blink at her. "What?"

"It *is* you." She breathes out, glances into the crowd and back to me. "It's been so long since…well, I guess I should have realized you'd be here."

Really?

"My dad said that you…well that there was more to your story. He said you gave up everything for the sake of justice."

Huh. That doesn't sound like me. But then again, maybe it does. I remember my father telling me I was born to solve crimes.

On the other hand, a different Booker called me a coward, told me I was running from who I was meant to be.

Maybe they were both right, but this version of me feels a little extreme, the pendulum swinging wildly the other direction.

Whatever the case, I do know this…Frankie will not die on my watch.

"I gave up everything because I had nothing else," I say in a low voice. I take her hand. "Let's go."

My plan is easy. I'll take her through the club. At some point, we'll get separated. I'll tell her to run.

And then, I will too.

I admit, there's not a lot of finesse to this strategy, but give me a break. I've only been here for four hours, and my head is still pounding, maybe a remnant of the concussion I experienced in my last lifetime.

Besides, I have other priorities that don't include Alexander Malakov and his scheme to build a Little Moscow. Maybe, if I can fix the watch, and figure out a way to go back, I can still save Eve.

And hold your horses, before you start bringing up my past failures. What I'm saying is let's just admit the truth. You change one thing in the past, and your entire present changes. I've seen it. You've seen it.

If I can stop Eve's murder, maybe I change things with the Russians too.

I'm willing to take my chances, if I can just stop Eve's murder.

"When I tell you, run," I say to Frankie as we venture onto the dance floor. The music is deafening, and bodies gyrate against us as we shove our way through the crowd. The smells are cloying— body odor, perfume, smoke, and beer. Oddly, Frankie has my hand in a death grip.

Nicki Minaj is rapping out "Yikes," and we're halfway across the floor when I hear it—sirens, shouts and the room turns bright as the lights flash on.

Police stream into the room wearing black vests and riot gear, armed, and shouting at party goers to put their hands up.

Which, no one does. Instead, chaos erupts and around me, people are pushing and shouting and I realize—

This is not a raid.

I've been in a police raid. It's not like in the movies, but rather a few plainclothes officers confronting dealers who they've already done business with.

This is a diversion. Shelby has sent the entire narcotics division to rescue me.

I pull Frankie close. "Run!" Then I let her go.

She vanishes into the crowd. I turn and make my way back to the stairs.

My cover is still intact if I play this right. Because maybe I don't fix the watch. Maybe I don't go back in time.

And if not, I need to bring down Alexander and his police-killing thugs.

Scrambling up the stairs, I beeline back to Alexander's office. The door is open and Alexander is standing in the room, staring down at the bedlam through two big windows. I grab his arm, spin him around.

He's so high he might not know me, so, "It's Staz. The police are raiding the place." And since he, too, knows a raid when he sees one, I add, "Probably retaliation for our war on cops."

I keep the growl out of my voice and add a little disgust. "I gotta get you out of here."

He nods and stumbles a little as I grab his arm and pull him down the hallway to an elevator.

It requires a thumbprint and I take a chance.

The door opens and I get in.

Roof or basement?

31

My instinctual guess is that Alexander has wheels downstairs, in the underground parking garage, so I punch the basement level.

He slumps against the wall and I use the opportunity to frisk him. I fish his keys from his pocket and yank him up as we move into the parking garage. It's not big, just a few vehicles, and when I hit the car finder button on the fob, I'm not surprised when a beautiful silver, late model Porsche 911 Carrera 4 convertible lights up.

Yeah, baby.

I settle him into the passenger seat and climb in behind the wheel. Run my hands on the leather steering wheel, my body sinking easily into the coupe seats.

The car practically reads my mind as it starts on its own, purring to life. I glance at Alexander, who is watching me. "Buckle up," I snap.

He grins, however, and says something in Russian. "*Sheeshka.*"

Sorry, pal, not my language.

But I grin back. Then grab the stick shift and peel out.

Apparently, there are some perks to the job I hadn't quite considered.

The parking garage gate opens, and I flick on the radio as we clear the building.

And Journey reminds me, "Don't Stop Believin'"

Maybe I won't.

CHAPTER 4

As I've jumped through time, I've come to understand myself.

Understand that, at my core, I'm always the same man, with the same passions, the same vices—certain things don't change.

This has given me a kind of stability. Like, the fact I drive—or drove—the same car for twenty years. And lived in the same house. And listened to the same music.

And loved the same woman.

Because I'm a man of predictability, I find myself parked outside my old craftsman home at 4 a.m..

The home Eve and I purchased when we found out we were pregnant with Ashley. She loved the original dark oak trim, the hardwood floors, and the backyard with the arching elm tree.

I cut that tree down during my last dance with the past, mostly because in a life that doesn't exist anymore, the tree fell and flattened the house.

In this world, the tree is gone. But the house still stands, and with it all the memories. Ashley, playing with her congregation of stuffed animals on the porch, her silly bear Gomer in the center. In my mind, she's seven—always seven—and wearing a pink dress, her hair in pigtails and she's singing to herself—"Let it Go"—from Frozen.

Maybe it's my subconscious telling me something my heart just can't hear. Let it go. In real time, she's been gone for nearly six weeks. Six. Weeks.

In this life, she never existed. Eve hasn't grown old with me. I haven't woken up with her body spooned against me, her curly red hair soft against my face. We haven't sat on the back porch of her family's home as the sun fell into the horizon beyond the lake. We haven't gone skinny-dipping under the stars.

We haven't worried over our daughter as she sat on an ER gurney, clutching Gomer and bravely receiving stitches after hitting her head at the park.

This life only exists in my head, and I have a deep and abiding fear that if I can't escape this world, this dark and brutal existence will overwrite those memories.

I will lose the girls I love yet again.

So I sit outside my old house in a Russian mobster's Porsche as the filaments of dawn stream across the sky in a hues of fire, just trying to breathe.

I don't know where else to go.

The Porsche's GPS system had a list of remembered locations and from that I found Alexander's home, a sprawling estate on, ironically, Lake Minnetonka, not too far from the Mulligans' place.

I dropped him off on his front steps, into the arms of his nighttime security (after dragging the gate code out of him.)

There's nothing pretty about a fifty-year-old man baked on coke.

I suppose there's also nothing pretty about a man who makes his living with his fists. I've already stared into that mirror. I'm not looking again.

Across the street from my house, a door opens and I'm surprised—but maybe not so much—to see my old neighbor, Gia emerge onto her porch. Her dark hair is tied back and she's wearing a headlamp and workout clothing. I'm thinking it's too dark to go for a run when her husband, Alex, comes out too. In all the versions of our lives, he's been a bit on the violent side, and my last memory of him was his sleeping off a bender on Gia's sofa while she made pancakes in my house.

Apparently, he's not that abusive man in this world. He's fit, is wearing compression shorts and a T-shirt, and is stretching out on the porch next to his wife. I see them smile at each other, and he even gives her a kiss on her forehead before they take off down the sidewalk, their headlamps parting the darkness.

I still ache everywhere, and watching this life continue without me makes me put the Porsche into gear and pull away from the life that's no longer mine.

I need sleep.

I need to wake up from this nightmare.

Most of all, I need answers. Which means my next stop is the home of Arthur Fox, watchmaker and time-travel expert. Or at least, dabbler in all things fourth-dimension related.

But it's too early to drive the one hour to Stillwater. I'd end up on his front doorstep before dawn, like a stalker.

Therefore, and because I'm a creature of habit, I drive to the only other place I've ever lived…the tiny one bedroom, third floor apartment in a walk-up brownstone on Holmes Ave, in Uptown.

As I pull up, I see the entire neighborhood has been renovated. My brownstone is gone, replaced by a sleek four-story building with tiny balconies and storefronts on the lower level.

I pull up in front of a bakery, with its back lights on, and the fragrance of fresh bread spilling out into the morning air, get out, and lock the Porsche.

Trying to get a feel for whether or not I live here, I stand for a long moment on the street. You'd think time might have mercy on a guy and not leave him homeless.

The lobby is locked, of course, but there's a touchpad by the door, both numbers and a scanner.

I take a chance and press my thumb to the scanner.

The door unlocks.

See. At the core, I don't change.

I open the inner door with the same thumbprint touch and find myself debating between the elevator and the stairs.

Stairs it is, and I head up to 302.

Another touch pad outside the sleek black door, and I hesitate for a moment. By all reason, this shouldn't work. But then again, none of this is reasonable, which means inside this door, I could find the current version of me.

What if I listen to hip-hop? Own a Prius?

What if I'm vegan?

The odds are against it, so I press my thumb to the door and it unlatches.

I stare into the room and feel like I've entered a portal to my soul, the dark world of a life without Eve's influence. She's been my better half for so long, I've forgotten where I end and she begins.

Is she the one who loves Bibimbap, or is that me? Is she the one who started us holding hands everywhere we go? Probably. What about our habit of reading aloud bits and pieces of magazine articles and excerpts of books at night? I might be able to own that one.

Eve is romantic, practical, smart—in my world, she was the head of her Crime Scene Investigations department. Breathtakingly beautiful, with shoulder length curly dark red hair and deep hazel-green eyes.

Eve loves to go barefoot, her feet propped on the dashboard of the convertible, eat pizza on the floor in front of the fire, and party on our back deck. *Let's paint the den yet another shade of white.*

The Rembrandt Stone before Eve was driven by justice, the need for fast cars and loud music, and the sense he had to put right what went wrong in the world. After Eve he was willing to slow down and breathe. She chiseled off the rough edges.

Those rough edges are back now, and quite apparent in an upgraded version of my bachelor apartment from twenty-three years ago. I walk into a room with industrial bookcases, contemporary black leather furniture, a sleek stainless-steel kitchen, black granite countertop, and a massive abstract oil painting of a blurred Minneapolis downtown-scape on one wall and an enormous flat screen on the other.

The view overlooks the same skyscape through an immense picture window.

My guess is I sit here, late at night, probably sleepless, staring out that window, my thoughts trending toward frustration.

Because, judging from the decor, I haven't changed much.

I drop the Porsche keys on the counter and walk to the fridge. As I suspect, a number of protein shakes line the door.

I grab one, and down it as I head to a king-sized bed in the bedroom. Setting the container on the side table, I strip off my soggy, grimy, smelly clothes and fall onto the bed.

The silk sheets are chilly against my skin and I roll on my side, grabbing the pillow and close my eyes.

I hate my life.

I dream snatches from timelines—a brother named Leonardo that I barely know, a fight with a man who haunts me, a cold night chopping down a tree, Eve's laughter weaving into my soul.

When I wake, the sun is up, but not far, and I'm raw, edgy and achy. A hot shower clears the cobwebs and by eight I'm back in the Porsche and heading south.

I first met Arthur Fox when John Booker bequeathed a box of cold case files to me after his death. At the bottom of the box lay a watch, the hands unmoving. I took the watch to Art, a retired watchmaker, who told me the watch was working, of course. He knew what it was even then.

How I wish he'd been wrong.

He lives in Stillwater, in a quaint two-story Tudor a couple blocks off main street. The first time around, the place was over-grown, he was a widower and he slammed the door in my face. He had buzzed-short gray hair, a lined face, and a permanent frown, so, like I've probably told you before, he wasn't the warmest coat in the closet.

Then I went back to the past and met his wife, Sheila, who gave me lemonade, and reminded me why every man needs a woman to soften his sharp edges. The second time we met, after I returned to my time, I found him in a wheelchair and knew, some-how, it was my fault.

During that visit, I met their daughter, Meggie, who shed some light on how my time travel worked. She called it Chrono-thesis, the ability to travel back in my mind, take over my younger body, and re-write the time stream.

I know, it sounds like science-fiction, but I've lived it now, so who am I to argue?

It was Art who warned me that one change to the past can ripple out in unintended and unimaginable ways. Fast forward twenty-three years and a couple time loops, and beautiful Meggie became victim thirty-eight of the Jackson killer's serial crime spree.

I still remember the picture of her taken at the crime scene—her body half-dressed, marks around her neck indicating strangulation. And, Art's words echo from another memory, a different time, before she died, when he found me at the police station, desperation in his voice, *"Have you found her?"*

I don't know. I hope when I ring the doorbell, I find him whole, his daughter restored and his wife making lemonade.

The house hasn't changed much. Built in the 1930s, the whitewash stucco looks recent, and the door is stained a dark brown. Monster hostas line the front walk, and a Japanese Maple is vibrant and starting the slow blush into autumn.

A couple geranium plants flank the door.

I take a breath and push the bell. It rings, the sound familiar, and matches the heavy thrum of my heartbeat.

He probably won't remember me—our last meeting, in his memory, was over twenty-three years ago, on a street in the suburbs, right after I'd totaled my Camaro and captured two drive-by shooters. I stopped them from T-boning his car, the accident that would have killed his wife and landed him in a wheelchair. But he'll never know that.

I dearly hope that Art and Sheila have lived happily ever after.

Footsteps, and I steel myself. He might not even live here anymore, but so far life hasn't moved that far off its axis.

The door opens. I smile.

A woman stands on the other side of the glass. She has shoulder length brown hair held back with a colorful headband, is wearing a pair of jeans and a gauzy top. Her glasses hang on a chain around her neck. "Hello?"

Sheila? She's aged since we last met, but I still recognize her. "Does Art Fox still live here?" I ask.

She nods, then turns and calls his name into the house.

My knees nearly buckle with relief.

She opens the door, then. "Would you like to come inside?"

I would, with everything inside me. I'm not sure why but seeing her, whole, still beautiful, tells me that maybe, finally, something turned out right.

I didn't accidentally dismantle their lives.

"Do I know you?" She puts on her glasses.

I debate, then finally, nod. "Inspector Rembrandt Stone."

"Right. *Rembrandt.* Wow, it's been ages. How are you?"

Her smile is like sunshine to my soul, a hot blast of hope that I can't dodge. I don't know why, but having someone know me—the me before I was Staz the Thug—fills my throat and I have the craziest, completely unnecessary urge to tear up.

Get ahold of yourself. It's just been a very, very long twenty-four hours.

Then Art appears. He looks better than I've ever seen him, well, in this era. He's wearing jeans and a T-shirt, is fit and tan—maybe from yard work. He holds out his hand to me. "How are you?"

How am I? Such easy words. Such a complicated answer.

I take his hand. "I'm not sure." Because, well, what would you say? "Actually, I'm having a problem with the watch."

Now, let's remember that Art knows about my time travel. He met younger me, back when I was trying to figure out how'd I'd chronothized, and I'd spilled everything.

And later, he knew I'd changed things. So, it comes as no surprise to me when he frowns. "What kind of problem?"

I take off the watch and hand it to him. "It's not working."

He looks at the watch, then back to me. "Have you tried turning the dial?"

I give him a look. He holds up his hand. "Right, okay. Let's take it back to my shop."

"Can I get you anything, Inspector?" Sheila asks, and for a moment I can't help but wonder where my parents are in this time. Do they think their son is a murderer?

"No, thanks, Sheila." I follow Art back to the small room he calls his office. It resembles an ancient surgical suite, with a high top table, a magnifying glass and a row of tiny instruments lined up.

He sits down on a tall chair and puts the watch on the table. Turns it over and pries off the back. "So, are you still living a double life?"

I really can't believe he knows this, but the answer is yes, in so many ways, so, "Unfortunately."

He looks over at me. "Someday, Rem, this will all come to an end, and it will be worth it."

I suddenly wonder if he's referring to Malakov or...or well, the real undercover life I live. The true lies I tell every day to the people in my life, on both sides of the timeline.

My confusion renders me mute, and I frown.

He leans back and turns in his chair. "You have to believe that what you are doing will turn out for good."

Again, I have no idea to what life he's referring. But I'll bite. I sit down in the only uncluttered chair. "I don't know. I feel like I'm just running in place. I fix something, and on the other side, lives go spinning out of control." I lean forward, my head in my hands. "She's gone, Art. My wife, Eve, is dead, and if I can't get this watch working, it's all over. I'll never be able to fix it."

He's silent, and I look up at him. He hasn't moved. "Maybe you aren't meant to fix it."

I frown at him. "No. You told me once that I have a responsibility to the one who gave me the watch to do the right thing. And...that's what I've been doing."

"So the question is…who gave you the watch?"

I sit up. "John Booker."

"Did he?"

I pause. "Yeah. Who else would it have come from? It came in a box of cold cases from his estate."

"Who managed his estate?"

I stare at him. "I don't know." I look at the watch. "And I never will. He's still alive. Or again, I guess. He's alive again."

He makes a sound and turns back to the watch, popping open the back. "Maybe the journey isn't about fixing things, but…the journey itself."

Thank you, Yoda.

I get up and come over to him, peering over his shoulder. "I don't care why I was given the watch. I just need it to work. Can you fix it?"

He's picked up one of his surgical instruments and prods the gears. They don't move. He makes another noise.

"What?"

"The gears are frozen." He tries to move one of them. "See, they're essentially fused together."

"Isn't that what they did before?"

"No, before the gears were movable, the watch just needed to be wound, with the right case file attached to give it direction. These gears almost act as if they're caught on something."

"Well, I'm here, and time has clearly progressed, so obviously that's not right."

He pushes the magnifying glass away. Turns to me. "What did you do?"

"Nothing. I mean—I didn't solve my last case…"

He's shaking his head and I don't want to say the other obvious idea, so, "What if I…what if I, um, *erased* someone…"

He raises an eyebrow.

I don't want to elaborate.

Silence passes between us. Then, "I think it's more than that. Something that goes against the watch's intent. It's almost as if you broke its soul."

Perfect. Now I'm the devil.

"Leave it with me," he says, "I'll see what I can figure out."

I glance at the watch, and it's not unlike he's asked me to leave my child behind for him to run tests on.

"I'll take good care of it." He touches my shoulder. "I promise."

I try a smile. Nod.

"Rembrandt. Be Stalwart."

He's using the words written on the back of the watch. I want to say I'm trying. But you and I both know I can't live in a world without Eve.

Sheila hands me a bag of homemade chocolate chip cookies on the way out.

I eat them all on my drive back to Minneapolis.

CHAPTER 5

By the time I enter Minneapolis city limits, Aerosmith's "Dream On" is pumping through all eight speakers of the Porsche's state of the art 150 watt Bose entertainment system, I have a crazy plan.

I blame it on the cookies, the sugar surging through my bloodstream. Clearly, I need to lay off the protein shakes.

Art will get the watch working. Some things you just have to believe.

Eventually, Booker will find a cold case for me to jump back to. In a city the size of Minneapolis, there has to be *something* on the books.

In the meantime, I will solve Eve's murder. I will scour her file, re-read every statement, comb through all the evidence. Since Leo Fitzgerald didn't kill her—I made sure of that—then someone else out there had a reason to want her dead. I'll search through all her past cases, all her courtroom testimonies, all her active files.

I will find her killer.

And then I will go back in time and save her. That's all that matters.

Whatever life I end up with will be the one that sticks.

I'm tired of this game. Tired of being stalwart. Tired of the journey.

From this moment on, I'm all about the destination.

I wish Burke was in my list of speed dials, and a fresh pang hits me. No more workouts at Quincy's. No more late-night jazz gigs, him at the drums, me holding down a table, trying to unravel the rhythms and beats of his choice of sound.

In one of the recent versions of this timeline, Burke had a daughter named Daphne, was married to Shelby. She was the Chief of Police.

I'm sorry, Burke. Whatever I did destroyed that beautiful life.

I feel a little sick. Could be the half dozen cookies I just consumed, but maybe not.

Disconnecting the Bluetooth from the car, I call Booker, just to check in on Frankie.

He answers on the second ring. "Why didn't you tell me?"

This is a lifetime that Booker has never been in, so I'm not used to the gravelly voice of age. It still contains, however, a hint of gunslinger in the tone and I take a beat before answering.

"I didn't know until I got there," I say, because I'm assuming he's referring to Frankie.

He is. "She could have been killed."

"You forget—I was there."

"Did you know about this?" He's almost accusatory, and maybe he's forgotten that I don't know about *anything*.

I imagine him standing at the window, one hand on his hip as he grips the phone as if he might be about to throw it.

"Of course, I didn't know about it," I snap. "I was as surprised as you were. She's your daughter, Booker. You're the only one to blame for her crazy ideas."

He hangs on up me.

I smile because Booker is back to his old self, and it's the first moment that I haven't felt like the world is imploding.

The feeling dissipates fast, however, and I redial him. "Where are you?"

"Frankie's house."

I know where she used to live, but just to be sure, "Little gray bungalow off Main Street in Hopkins?"

"That's the one."

Now I hang up. I turn up the radio. The oldies station is playing REO Speedwagon, "Take It On The Run," and I punch up the volume as I head west on 36.

At 443 horsepower, the car has a deep, throaty hum, and just for fun, I zip around a few cars, just to see how she handles. I bring her back down to the speed limit before I can draw any attention, but I'm in love.

I'm keeping this car.

I get on 35W, and head toward downtown, the sun sparkling off the IDS Tower and the beautiful black roof of the U.S Bank Stadium. I wonder if the Vikings have won any conference championships in this timeline.

Maybe in this world, they've even nabbed the Vince Lombardi, and if that's the case, I sort of hate to take that away.

But some things are worth any price.

Kenny Loggins sings about the "Danger Zone," as I clear downtown, staying on 35W to Lake. Then I get off and troll through the old beat neighborhood until I get to Calhoun. I remember a rumor that they'd recently changed the name, but I can't remember, Calhoun being etched into my fifty-plus-year-old brain.

I open her back up a bit on 7, but keep from getting too crazy, and finally turn into downtown Hopkins.

Frankie's house is a cute one and a half-story with the garage in the back and an awning over the front stoop. I park at the curb, and wonder a moment what the neighbors will think, and then decide I don't care and get out.

So much for laying low.

But my guess is that the cops around here know me, or at least what I'm up to, especially if Shelby is boss. Which, if Booker has retired, is probably the case.

At least that's the hand time dealt her last go round.

I knock on the door but it opens before I can finish and Frankie is there. She's wearing a pair of shorts and a baggy T-shirt, and only now do I see how much she resembles Booker—same steely gray eyes, same fierce expression. She looks past me, scanning the street, then motions me inside.

"Seriously? You're going to get me killed!"

I glance at the Porsche, back to her. "I'll tell Alexander I'm following up."

"On what—killing me?" She has her hands on her hips, her eyebrows up and I admit, maybe I'm not thinking this all the way through.

I have other things on my mind, and maybe Booker knows this because like a bouncer, he trots over to Frankie from where he was sitting at an island perched between the main room and the kitchen and puts a hand on her shoulder. "Calm down. Rem's had a long night."

"Calm down?" She turns to her father. "The Brotherhood has put out a death threat against you, Dad. You." She shakes her head. "You need to start taking this seriously."

I look at him. "Why you?"

He lifts a shoulder. "Probably because I put Boris Malakov in jail twenty years ago. He got out about six months ago."

"Well, that's a reason," I say.

Frankie turns to me. "You want to know why I was there? Because my father doesn't seem to care that he's getting ma—"

"Frankie, that's enough." Booker says in his Old West sheriff's voice.

"No." She walks over to her laptop, sitting on the counter and punches in a code. The screen lights up. "I downloaded all the data on Malakov's phone while I was in his office—"

"You what?" I join her at her computer. Files fill the screen. "What is this?"

"All the data he stores on his cloud drive." She looks at me. "I knew if I got inside Malakov's office, an alarm would go off and eventually, Malakov would show up, probably with his cell phone in his pocket. I just needed five minutes with him close enough for my phone to connect to his signal, and activate the program I wrote—"

I stare at her. "Who *are* you?"

She grins at me. "Impressed, Inspector Stone?"

Huh. I nod twice and turn to Booker. "How did this happen?"

He frowns, and I don't want to go into the details, but, "I thought you wanted to be a reporter when you grew up."

"Where did you ever get that?" she says. "I wanted to be a cop like my dad." She grins at him. "I work for the Cybercrime department."

Booker rolls his eyes.

I agree. "What if I hadn't come along? What if Vita decided to question you, himself?"

"I had backup," she says simply and looks away.

Silence.

"I'm waiting."

She folds her arms, like a toddler refusing to budge. Apparently

I'll have to put the screws to her to get any answers.

"I don't know where she gets it," Booker says, but he's grinning.

I'm not. "It's Zeke. Zeke's your backup."

She looks at me. "Zeke? Zeke who?"

"Seriously?" I give her a look.

"Okay, fine." She glances at her father.

"What does Zeke have to do with this…?" Booker's still confused, but that doesn't stop the steam pouring from his ears as he puts together the pieces. It's only a second before—

"You're *dating* Zeke Kincaid?" he roars.

Oops. Now, before everyone freaks out, let me say that Zeke is a good guy. The son of a perp I arrested back in time, I checked in on him over the years and he sort of followed in my footsteps. Which may or may not have been a good idea, but here we are.

"Dad, listen—" Frankie says.

"No." He holds up a hand. "Zeke is trouble. He plays a little too loose with the rules, and he's going to get you hurt."

Not unlike what Danny said about me.

Maybe Booker is right. Danny sure turned out to be, in the end.

But I know Zeke. "Booker. Zeke is a good guy—"

"How would you know?" He's rounded on me.

I put up my hands. "I just know. From…before. From other…jobs. Zeke is—"

"Your protégé."

Oh. Huh.

"Don't think I didn't know you were in his life, growing up, even when you went dark. Or that you recruited him into your underworld after he joined the force."

I did? Great. But like I said, I have some core behaviors that don't seem to change.

And frankly, I'm just a little relieved that I didn't just turn into a complete jerk. Aren't you? That a little of the old Rembrandt survived, even without Eve.

"Where was he?" I ask Frankie about her, quote, *backup.*

"He was in the crowd in the nightclub," she says. "I found him after you told me to run."

My mouth is a tight line. Zeke is playing a dangerous game and I hope it doesn't blow up on us.

"So, what did the phone files tell you?"

"I don't know yet. I'm still trying to figure out how to get past the encryption." She turns back to the computer. "Get that Porsche off my front yard before you get me killed and I'll text you when I have something."

I like her. She reminds me, in a way, of Eve.

And now I remember why I'm here. I gesture to Booker and he walks over.

"Please tell me you found a cold case."

His grim face sets a fist in my chest. "I searched all your files. There's nothing between the shooting from Jin's Liquors and the next case, the woman we found in the Mississippi River in June of '98."

I remember that case. The woman had been missing for six years when we found her.

He cuts his voice low. "You can't go back past the case you just solved."

"But I didn't solve the liquor store shooting. There was another perp—I know there was. I saw him in the driver's seat."

He sighed. "Yeah, well, with all the horror of Eve's murder, the case simply got closed."

"Maybe that's why time stopped."

He frowns at me.

"I went to see Arthur Fox." A slow smile crosses his face, and I *knew* it. "You know him too. You visited him."

He nods. "Back when I first got the watch, I had a…well, a glitch."

He mentioned that before, and I glance at Frankie, but she's got her head down and is deep into her hacking.

"What kind of glitch?"

He sticks his hands into his pockets. "Not so much a glitch as a question."

"An ethical question. You changed something, didn't you?"

He grimaces. "Maybe. Back in my early days. When I was young and idealistic and—"

"What did you change, Booker?" I take a step closer, and he doesn't move. And I know. "This has something to do with me." I frown. "Listen, if you're talking about Mickey's murder, and the fact that you went back and found him, I know about that. I know you couldn't stop it—I get it." I put my hand on his shoulder. "It's done. And, by the way, my parents had another son, Leonardo, and he's a great kid. I blame you for that."

I give him a smile, but he doesn't echo it.

I drop my hand. "What?"

He glances at Frankie, then heads for the door and steps outside.

Oh wow. It's that kind of conversation.

If he were still a smoker, he'd be reaching for a pack. As it is, he walks out into Frankie's yard, starts kicking at some weeds lodged between the cracks of her cement walk. "I changed something."

Well, I'd figured that much, but I'm silent to his confession.

"I caused…Mickey's death."

I fix my eyes on Booker.

This, I did not expect.

A moment passes between us as I try to process his words. Here's what you should know. When I was twelve, my brother Mickey and I were out biking. I'll admit I was slightly annoyed that he was following me, yet again, but at age nine, that's what little brothers do. So I sped up. I was so far up the road I didn't see a white van pull over. Someone opened the door and yanked Mickey off his bike while I was 100 feet ahead, putting on steam. Forty years later, I still can't forgive myself.

Originally, he wasn't found for another seventeen years when his body was recovered by some fisherman in a lake near our house. As you can imagine, it destroyed our family. And ignited my desire to be a cop.

That's the reality I know, the one I lived. The one I thought was the original.

The more current reality is one where Booker, via our time-traveling watch, used my brother's cold case and caught the murderer shortly after he dumped my brother's body in the lake.

It set my parents free, in a way, from the death-grasp of living with ambiguity. Closing the case allowed them to move on, and last time we met, they'd not only healed, but added another brother to our family. Never mind that he's named Leonardo, an eerie shadow to the serial killer I've spent six weeks and twenty-plus years chasing.

I like Leo. He's smart, reminds me of Mickey, and we're pals.

Like I told Booker, he's to thank for this happyish ending. How could he have been the cause of my brother's murder, so many years ago? "I don't understand."

He glances up at me, wearing a face I recognize.

Regret.

"When I first got the watch from my boss, Greg Sulzbach, I did the same thing you did. I pulled out the case I regretted the most…the murder of a young mother and her son during my rookie year on the force." He's kicked free the weeds from the crack and now reaches down to pick up the debris. "It was a terrible crime—a woman found beaten to death, and her nine-year-old son, also killed. We suspected the father, but couldn't make it stick, as he had a solid alibi. But in my gut, I knew it was him." He walks over to the trash bin in Frankie's driveway and throws the debris inside. The cover falls with a clunk.

He turns, dusting off his hands, then meets my eyes. "I went back to the moment of her death with the intent of catching the man in the act of murdering his son."

I nod.

"I was right. He *had* lied about his alibi. In my original timeline, I'd done a drive-by moments before, so I arrived blocks away just a few minutes after his wife died, while he was hunting through the house for his son. He was high on meth, angry and violent and we had an altercation that resulted in his death. But I made it in time."

I swallow, my breath tight in my chest. "The boy lived."

He nodded, looked away, his mouth a grim line. His shoulders rose, fell. "He grew up to be a psychopathic murderer who, a couple decades later, pretended to be an ice cream man and killed young boys around the Twin Cities metro area, and beyond."

"Donald Simmons." The name is from a previous timeline, and I'm surprised I remember it. But Booker nods, so I must be right.

"If I hadn't saved him, he wouldn't have killed your brother."

Yeah, I know, my mind is blown too. Because what he's saying is that theres a timeline I don't remember. An original before mine. A timeline in which…Mickey lived.

Suddenly it all makes sense. Booker's almost rabid commitment to the rules of the watch. No changing the past.

Still, "If you knew how changing things would create another tragedy, why did you go back and grab Simmons when he dumped Mickey's body?"

He looks at me now. "That was different. I didn't save anyone, did I? I followed the rules, solved the case, and kept your family from experiencing seventeen years of anguish."

His eyes hold compassion, and maybe apology and it's a weird mix that I don't know what to do with. However, I understand it far too well, having been the man who somehow let a serial killer loose to murder thirty-eight women.

"You did that for me," I say, with a ping of understanding. "Because you saw it break me."

He lifts a shoulder. "I did what I could and tried to live with the rest."

I'm not sure why, but his simple words lodge inside me. This is my problem. I can't live with the rest.

But maybe I'll have to. "When I talked to Art, he told me the watch's gears were frozen. He thinks it's because something happened that went contrary to the watch's intent." And, let's not forget that, according to Art, I broke its *soul*.

Booker frowns. "The watch is meant to solve crimes. To find justice…"

"So what if, somehow, I…created a cold case."

And you know what I'm talking about—Leo's murder, right?

He's looking at me, and I have no choice. "I killed Leo Fitzgerald."

"Rem. I know. You told me last night—but what you clearly don't remember is that you were exonerated for that years ago. You claimed self-defense and the evidence supported it. That case is solved."

Shoot. I was so hoping that might be the case we could use.

Now, I run a hand across my mouth, and stare out at the Porsche.

There has to be a case I can use.

I let out a long breath. "What about Eve's case?"

"You know the rules. You'll arrive after she dies—"

"No, I'll arrive when she's *taken*. When the crime is first committed. I might have time—"

He's looking at me like he wants to believe me. And I know I sound desperate, but, "Maybe he didn't kill her right away. She did call me, and I called her back…"

But he's shaking his head. "Coroner put her time of death shortly after she called you. I don't know, Rem—"

"Then I just have to find out where she was taken."

"No, that won't work. You'll go back to where you were at the time. Asleep on her sofa." He raises his eyebrow.

"Seriously? I'd just suffered a dislocated shoulder and was nursing a concussion. I'd gone to her house to wait for her." I closed my eyes, thinking. "She was working late, so she must have been taken from police headquarters."

"I don't think so. No one saw her return after going to the hospital with you that night."

That's right—my sketchy memory is returning. I'd ended up in the hospital after running down a suspect from the shooting at Jin's Liquors. He'd taken a header into an oncoming vehicle at a monster truck rally, so Shelby recruited me to break the news to his parents. After I got my shoulder reset, under Eve's watchful eyes, we left the hospital.

I never saw Eve again.

"Who would take her? Was it personal?" I ask.

Booker shakes his head. "I didn't run the investigation—we

left that to Shelby and Burke."

I still.

"Rem, like I said last night—you were in no shape to run that investigation."

I suppose not. I have seen myself before in a life without Eve and it isn't pretty.

"I need to talk to Shelby. Get the file."

"I can get you the file, probably, but as for talking to Shelby…"

I freeze. "Please don't tell me she's dead."

He recoils. "What—no. Why would you say that?"

I hold up my hand. "Trust me on this, it's happened before." And no, not Shelby, but you know what I mean. If you were me, you might jump to conclusions too.

"Shelby lives in Florida. But her number is unlisted. She's still a cop, last I heard."

Huh. "Where?"

"Miami."

I know one thing—if I'm going to save Eve, I'm going to need to solve her murder *before* I show up in the past.

"Find me her address," I say, and head toward my Porsche. "And text it to me."

"Where are you going?" Booker has walked out to the edge of the lawn, by the sidewalk.

I open the door to the Porsche and look back at Booker. He looks old standing there, his shoulders stooped, his jeans baggy. Life has taken its toll on him, but in his countenance, I still see the lawman considering me. Measuring, and I hear his words. *I did what I could and tried to live with the rest.*

Like I already told you, I'm not ready to live with the rest.

"I'm going to talk to Shelby."

CHAPTER 6

The last thing I said to Eve, in our previous lifetime, was that I'd move to Florida with her and become a surfer.

She laughed. I can still hear it sometimes. And then she said yes to marrying me.

As I drive north, out of Miami, toward the address on Golden Beach that Booker texted me, it's the only thing I can think about.

That and the fact that the last time I was in Miami, Leo Fitzgerald tried to drown me in the middle of the Atlantic, and would have succeeded if Eve and Burke hadn't tracked me down and saved my life.

So, there's a couple brutal memories to keep me motivated, despite my sleep-deprived state.

However, the sun is bright, and the sky is so brilliantly blue overhead, it feels like I could dive into it. To my right, the ocean is rolling onto the shore, not quite violent, but not calm, either, just an eternal rhythm that lifts spray into the air. The top is down on the Camaro I rented, the wind fresh in my short hair, Boston is singing, "Don't Look Back," and I'm wearing a pair of jeans, my Cons and a palm tree patterned shirt I picked up at the airport.

I'm hoping hard that Shelby remembers details, even hunches from the case because the file that Booker uploaded, and that I read on my phone on the plane, told me little.

Eve was found at four a.m. at Minnehaha Park after an extensive search. She'd been dead for roughly six hours, almost immediately after she'd been taken. The coroner reported marks of a struggle—a bruise on her face, maybe where she'd been hit, and a nail broken on her hand. Her knuckles were bruised, as if she'd gotten a lick in, too. My gorge rises at the images that brings up in my mind.

My tough Eve, battling for her life.

Like Booker said, she'd been strangled, with deep bruises on her throat, and even into the well of her neck, but not sexually assaulted.

Her body was locked inside a 1977 Oldsmobile Toronado. An *Oldsmobile Toronado*. I sit on that for a long time, my gut churning.

Leo Fitzgerald's stepfather owned a Toronado, and just hours before her death, we'd pegged a Toronado as the vehicle used to run down Eve's best friend, Julia Pike, some fifteen years prior.

It couldn't possibly be the same car.

And besides, like I've mentioned, I killed Leo. He couldn't have been around to kill Eve.

My gut is still a mess as I drive, mulling over the report.

Shelby interviewed everyone at the police station, and no one saw Eve return. Her car, a Ford Escort, was found a few blocks away from the station, parked in front of a church, her satchel on the sidewalk.

Someone had called in 911 with the news of her abduction off the street.

Somewhere between parking her car and heading into

headquarters, she was taken.

And murdered.

The Toronado was wiped clean—not a fiber to be found. And no DNA on her body. She was wearing a winter jacket, jeans and boots, and the coroner found nothing on her clothing either.

In Shelby's interview of Silas he mentioned me, and how she'd left the investigation of Bianca Potter, a woman who'd been killed the night before in downtown Minneapolis, to join me at the hospital. By the tone of it, Silas clearly wanted my name on the list of suspects.

My sad alibi is that, like Booker said, I was asleep on her sofa. And apparently Shelby did question me, but by the report she gave of our finding Eve's body, it's clear she crossed off my name.

I read that report with some trepidation.

Booker's right—they tracked Eve down via her cell phone. Her last call had been to me and was in her pocket when she was taken. When we found her, apparently time repeated itself. I made a mess of the crime scene, grabbing her, trying to administer CPR, falling apart. I even had it out with Danny Mulligan, her father, when he showed up.

I know he's a cop, and he should have known better, but let's go a little easy on the younger me, okay? I had found a woman who loved me, despite my quirks, my passions and frankly, I nursed a bit of an anger issue back then.

That's what happens when you can't escape the sense that life is out to destroy you.

I'm not sure I've escaped it, even now.

I certainly don't know what I did to the Almighty to get him on my bad side. *I did what I could, and tried to live with the rest.* Booker's words, and I get it.

Me too, sort of. But clearly, I didn't get it right.

I *will* get it right. Figure out how to get the watch working, and fix everything. Don't look at me like that. This time it'll work. Really.

For the record, I like Florida. I would have gladly become a surfer for Eve. Although we couldn't have afforded the slick and modern two-story homes that line Ocean Boulevard as I head north. Probably, we would have found a small two bedroom in the suburbs, something my detective salary could manage.

I know without a doubt we would've been happy.

I'm not sure Booker has the address right. I'm in the thick of beach side mansions in the double-digit millions on one side of the road, and high-rise condos for a cool mill on the other side. The road is divided, with a greening boulevard of palm trees down the center, and when my GPS dings, I have to turn around at a light, and head back.

Here, the traffic is slower, the driveways gated, the architecture cutting edge, cement buildings with two-story windows, built skinny and tall to overlook the ocean across the street. Nothing of the comfort and warmth of my vintage craftsman…

That I no longer own.

I tap the brakes in front of a house that could double for an office building, save for the rooftop garden and black house numbers running vertically down the stuccoed white wall. A wooden canopy arches over a long walkway and the house is set back, behind a white paver-set drive.

In the driveway sits a turquoise blue Maserati GranTurismo.

The gate is open. What looks like the truck of a cable guy sits in the front, a ladder affixed on top and the side door open.

I pull in. Glance at the van. No movement inside, so I get out, and head toward the door. It's down a long walk, with palm trees growing up on either side of the portico, and as I move into shadow, the heat dissipates from my body.

I almost feel a chill, like this is not right.

Not at all.

I get to the door and touch the bell.

Hear nothing.

That's when something cold presses to the back of my skull. "You shouldn't be here."

It's a woman's voice, and I raise my hands, my heart jolting. "Shelby?"

A pause, and I turn my head.

"Stop."

"Shelby it's me—Rem—"

"Why are you here?"

Okay, not at all the greeting I'd expected, but fair question. After all, I did kill the man she loved. Or at least that's the story on the street. "I need to talk to you about Eve's case."

A pause, then. "That's all?"

I frown. "Why else?"

She's silent for a moment. "Were you followed?"

This time I'd been careful. "No."

A deep sigh, and finally the lethal end of her weapon leaves its perch. I turn.

This is not the Shelby I took under my wing as a rookie and trained. That Shelby was, well, not *this* Shelby.

That Shelby had long blonde hair, legs that didn't quit and a way about her that had made Burke forget his own name.

This woman is still stunning, but her hair is cut almost military short, a golden cap that's all business. She's tan, her eyes still impossibly blue, and she's wearing a black half-tee that shows off some pretty impressive abs, a pair of white jeans and white Cons.

And she's holding a 9mm Ruger like she means it. She slips

on the safety and looks at me, those blue eyes sharp. "Really?" Her lips are pursed.

"Really what?"

"You flew all the way down here to ask me what I've already put in my report? Don't you know that just you showing up here is dangerous?"

Funny, Asher said the same thing.

"No one is going to get hurt. I'll jump back on a plane tonight, and no one will be the wiser." Besides, I hardly think the game I'm playing in Minneapolis is going to find its way to Florida.

"Get inside," she says with a shake of her head and motions to her front door, which she unlocks with a remote she pulls from her pocket.

"Nice place," I say as I step over the threshold. I'm not just being polite. The place is massive, with a soaring, three-story entry, balconies overlooking the vestibule. A floating stone staircase with glass rails zags up the middle of the otherwise open interior. The three-story window lets in light from the street onto a seating area with white leather sofas and mid-century modern turquoise blue accent chairs, all surrounding what I hope is a fake zebra rug over the poured cement floors.

Opposite that, a massive glass dining table—maybe twelve chairs around it—sits in front of yet another three-story window that overlooks a huge rectangular pool.

The place is clean, smells faintly of lemon and lavender, and if I breathe hard, I think I might hear it echo off the ceiling.

"This way," Shelby says and walks past me, down a hallway, into another part of the house. Through tall double doors we enter what I'm guessing is her home office.

I want this office. In another life, I was an author, and I had an oh-so-inspiring view of my kitchen.

This office faces the spectacular crystalline blue pool. A clear acrylic desk sits in the center of the room over a cow hide, a couple modern wicker chairs in front of it. Behind the transparent desk is a black credenza with three massive flat screens affixed to the wall.

Another door leads off it to an interior room. It's spotless.

As I approach the desk, Shelby scoots in front of me and slaps her laptop shut.

"This place is incredible, Shelby."

She gestures to a wicker chair and sits in the molded white leather one at her desk. "Thanks."

I want to ask her how she can afford this all on a cop's salary. I mean really, either Miami has really upped their budget or—

"I got this place from a client."

I frown.

"He'd hired me to follow his wife and I caught her cheating with his business partner. He didn't want her getting anything in the divorce, so he signed the house and his car over to me before he filed."

A *client.* "Are you a PI?"

She smiles, the first one I've seen, and something in her seems to relax. "Yes. A high-end one. I'm not in the yellow pages, for obvious reasons."

Obvious reasons? I'm about to ask what she specializes in when she leans forward, her hands folded on her desk, like I might be a client. "What can I do for you, Rem?"

"Like I said, I'm looking into Eve's case, and I need to fill in some blank spaces."

"Why now, Rem?" She shakes her head. "It took you so long to get over it. Why open the case now?"

"Because it's still cold!" And yeah, I didn't mean to raise my voice, but well, this is Shelby.

Once upon a time, she trusted me. Trusted my hunches.

Had my back.

I'm hoping she still does.

She holds up her hand. "Okay, I get that. I failed you, I know. I'm so sorry." She sighs. "After Burke was shot, it all fell apart for me, too." She leans back and looks out, toward the pool. "Frankly, I had to get away. To put it behind us. To start over. And Eve's case just…"

"Fell off your radar," I say, recognizing the Shelby I knew, the one who'd been Eve's best friend. Her death had to tear her up, too.

"I still have nightmares of those six hours," she says, getting up. She goes over to a cabinet in the wall, presses and a door opens.

A fridge. She takes out a bottled water and puts it on the table in front of me, grabs one for herself. "You were so frantic—we all were." She stares down at the bottle. "And then, when you found her…"

She looks past me, out toward the pool, and her eyes fill. "I'd seen grief up close, but never like what it did to you, Rem. It was…" She tightens her mouth. Shakes her head and when she looks back at me, a tear makes it down her cheek. "I tried to stop you, but you went crazy. You grabbed her out of the car and put her on the ground and started doing CPR, right there in the snow. She was blue, clearly dead for a while, but you kept breathing for her, trying to get her heart pumping. And then, when you figured out it wasn't going to work, you just sort of…" Her jaw tightens. "You made a sound. Like you'd lost part of your soul, maybe."

I'm staring at her. I knew young me loved her, but…apparently, I had no idea how much.

"Unfortunately, the crime scene was torn up. When Burke arrived, you were still holding her in your arms, and it was Danny who finally tore you away. Of course, you and he went at it, but it was grief, and we all knew it."

Okay, she's right, this isn't helpful at all.

"Did you run the plates on the Toronado?"

"There were no plates. And the VIN number was scratched off. We got a partial on it, but nothing panned out."

"No prints?"

"Wiped clean." She takes a drink of her water. "I finally got you back into the car, and you watched from there as they processed the scene. It took three hours before they removed her body, and then you followed her to the morgue. You were in pretty bad shape, with your dislocated shoulder, and Burke and I got you home while we waited for the autopsy. I think we were there until the next day."

"You stayed with me that whole time?"

"Not just me. Burke, too. He was really worried."

Burke. The mention of him stirs another deep ache.

"He was a good cop," I say. "And a good friend."

She smiles at that, something sad in her eyes.

Then I wind back her words from earlier. Us. Put it behind *us*.

"Shelby, who is—"

"Mom! I got it!" The voice singsongs down the hallway, and I freeze.

Mom?

Shelby glances toward the door.

Into her office walks a girl, about fifteen years old. Beautiful bronze skin, kinky blonde hair, clearly dyed, and dark at the edges, wearing a summer dress and sandals. She's waving a piece of paper when she enters, then stops.

"You passed! Congratulations!" Shelby says, not sounding at all like the woman who just held a gun on me.

But the teenager's gaze is on me. "Sorry. I didn't realize you were with a client."

"Actually, honey, this is…an old friend." Shelby walks over, and slips her arm around her daughter. "Rembrandt, this is Daphne. Honey, this is my old partner, Rembrandt Stone."

Daphne. I want to thank fate for that kindness. At least Shelby and Burke's daughter survived the time-travel calamity of the last round.

"Oh," she says quietly. "Um, nice to meet you, Mr. Stone."

She's tall and willowy and I see my friend Burke in her features.

But now I'm very confused. Although if Shelby was pregnant with her before Burke died…

Us.

I stand up.

"Roads, beware," says a voice. "It's a good thing I can't drive or I'd be afraid to go out on the streets."

And then I see him. Andrew Burke, back from the so-called dead, appearing in the doorway of Shelby's office.

He's holding a white cane, a sharp contrast to his dark skin. He looks good, lean, muscled, his head bald. He's wearing a white linen shirt and a pair of black dress pants and sandals, and sunglasses, like a man of leisure.

Except, he doesn't remove his glasses, and one more glance at the cane, and the way he brailles into the room, stopping by the edge of the doorway, tells me why.

"Burke," I say, on a thread of breath.

His mouth opens, and the room quiets, just us, reeling in time. "Rembrandt."

He's alive. Blind, but Andrew Burke is very much alive.

"Mmmhmm." I walk over, and I'm stupidly blinking back heat in my eyes. "I thought you were dead."

He makes a sound, almost of confusion, and then reaches out

for me.

I grab his hand, and then step close, swing my arm around his neck. Yes, I'm that guy now, and I don't care.

He apparently feels the same, and he slaps my back a couple times before letting me go. "What are you doing here?"

Same thing Shelby asked me, but nicer this time. I glance at her, back to Burke. "I needed to talk to Shelby about Eve's case."

He makes another noise, then, "Daphne, Rem and I need to talk, can you give us a minute."

She's still standing with her mother, still looking at me like she might be seeing a ghost, or perhaps the thief her mother mistook me for, but she nods. "I want to go for a swim, anyway. Nice to meet you," she says to me, softly, as she leaves.

An awkward silence descends.

"So," Burke says quietly. "Is it over?"

I haven't a clue what he's talking about.

"Have you brought down the Brotherhood in Minneapolis? Put the Malakov brothers behind bars?"

Oh. That's what I was up to. "Not yet."

He frowns. "Okay, then…um.."

"He wasn't followed," Shelby says, coming over to Burke, her hand on his shoulder. "I asked, plus I have Jorge doing a security sweep. We're clear."

Burke swallows, but nods.

I can't help myself. "Why did Booker say you were dead?"

"Really?"

"I mean, I've been under a while. I just resurfaced, and I thought…well, I was worried."

I'd say all of that is true, wouldn't you?

Shelby runs her hand down his arm, looking at him with sadness in her eyes. "Well, I suppose, to the world he is, because yes,

Andrew Burke was gunned down by his partner in an accidental shooting." Her tone contains no malice.

Still, I tense.

"You still don't remember?" Burke says, however, maybe sensing my racing heartbeat.

I shake my head. "It's still fuzzy."

"You didn't shoot me, Rem," Burke says. "You were hit, your gun stolen and Boris Malakov used it to shoot me."

He can't know the relief that gusts out of me. Or maybe he can because he smiles. "Really? All this time—?"

"I didn't ask enough questions, clearly."

Shelby puts her hand on my shoulder. Squeezes. I feel forgiveness in her touch.

"We thought it was the only way to get you inside the Brotherhood's organization," Burke said. "You said—let's use this tragedy for the sake of justice."

"So. Boris Malakov shot you," I say, taking a chance. "And I was framed for it."

"Yes," Burke said. "And you helped Booker put him away for murder. However, if anyone knew I was still alive, Boris would probably find a way to finish the job, so maybe, just in case, Booker kept up the lie, to keep us all safe."

"Until the traitor handed out our address," Shelby says, letting Burke go. "Want some water, honey?"

Burke shakes his head and walks over to a wicker chair with a practiced step.

I glance at Shelby, who shuffles over behind Burke. No wonder she held me at gunpoint. For all she knew, I came here to finish the job. "I'm so sorry. I didn't mean to put you two in jeopardy."

"We're okay. We have a new life, a new identity, and outside you and Booker, no one knows we're alive."

Not quite the happy ending I would have wanted for my best friend but it's better than him being dead.

Much better.

"Why does Malakov want you dead?"

He frowns, and my guess is that I should know this, so, "I mean, after all this time, one would think that he'd let the past go."

"I wouldn't forgive someone for killing my son, even if it was accidental." He shakes his head. "If I could go back in time, I'd tell my younger self to wait for backup."

I lodge those words in my brain, just in case.

"Are you sticking around? I'm playing down on the strip tonight."

"Playing?"

"The drums." He grins and Shelby leans down and kisses him.

"Sticks Malone, best jazz drummer in Miami," she says, looking at me, her eyes warm. I'm remembering a double date back in the day when these two first fell in love.

Those were good days.

Burke's smile falls. "So, you're still working for Alexander Malakov?"

"Yes. And he's recently started a range war in Minneapolis. We think he has something big planned, and I'm trying to figure it out before it happens."

"Using your infamous hunches?" Burke asks, and I'm not sure if he's mocking me or not. "They sure got you into trouble."

And, saved lives. But I don't add that.

"You were a good detective, Rem," Shelby says. "One of the best. You found things that I never saw. Like that twenty we found in the back of the car. You said it was linked to her murder—"

"What twenty?"

I'm looking at her, clearly something of horror on my face

because she frowns. "It's in the list of evidence—I'm sure of it."

I'll need to read the file again. Maybe my exhausted brain skipped over it. "Did it have any writing on it?"

"Writing?"

"The words, *Thank you for your service.*"

"Like the one on that hooker, Delaney," Burke says.

Good memory, Burke. "Yes."

Shelby shakes her head. "I'm sorry, Rem, I don't remember. Maybe. You were really freaking out and maybe it got ignored or dismissed in the wake of securing her body. You could check the files."

Who knows if CSI flagged it. But certainly, if I said it was linked to her murder—

Oh Booker, you should have let me work the case!

Still, all this has me stymied. This *can't* be a Jackson case, the serial killer who left a twenty-dollar bill with his victims, those words written in black Sharpie on the back. Why? Because I tracked down the Jackson killer. And sure, I cheated—I found him in the present, then went back to the past to stop his killing sprees—but I found him all the same. And, well, you know…killed him.

He couldn't have been Eve's murderer.

Unless, and I realize now I'm breathing heavily.

Unless I was wrong.

If I close my eyes, I can hear him, Leo Fitzgerald, right before the fight that ended his life. *"It's not me!"*

Ironically, they were almost the same words he used twenty-three years later, and a lifetime earlier, on a boat off the shore of Miami. *"I didn't do nothing to either of those girls."*

But it's not his words of denial that suddenly stand out, but Eve's. *But, Rem. What if this isn't the guy?*

I sink into the chair opposite Burke.

"Are you okay?" he asks, clearly still able to see me, despite his blindness.

"No, I'm not." My gut is reeling.

"What?" Burke says, his voice soft, but insistent.

"I don't know. I might have been wrong."

"About what?"

I swallow, hard and deep. "I think I might have made a horrible mistake."

If you're following along, and the facts are right, then, well, it's pretty obvious, isn't it?

Leo Fitzgerald was not the Jackson killer.

For all I know, that killer is still at large.

The room is suddenly spinning and I think I might be ill.

Burke leans over and put his hand on my knee. "Listen, I got your back, bro. You can 9 Line me anytime."

I look up at him, and he doesn't seem to be kidding. Wait. "Burke. The other night…did *you* get my emergency call?"

Shelby is looking down at him, then at me. "Oh, please, don't tell me you two are still—"

"Did it work?" He's grinning. "I thought maybe calling in the cavalry might do the trick."

"You saved my backside."

He leans back and lifts a shoulder. "Yeah, well, that's what partners are for."

I suddenly regret every moment I left Burke out in the cold, every dodge I made, not telling him the truth about my time travel. How would things be different if he'd known, right from the get go?

Next time around, if there is a next time, things will be different.

I promise.

CHAPTER 7

Where is my car?

I'm not surprised to get this text as I step off the plane this afternoon in Minneapolis. After all it is a Porsche 911.

I'd be wondering where my ride was, also, if someone had swiped it for two days. But I don't answer Alexander as I walk through the parking garage. It's raining, the sky a dismal gray and the air is muggy in the July heat.

Maybe I shouldn't have stayed overnight with Burke and Shelby, but I couldn't resist the lure of the old friendship. To know Burke still has my back seemed to settle the sense that I'm living far from myself in this lifetime.

Their daughter Daphne is smart, witty and laughed over a few stories I told of her father, back in the days before all this chaos started. We shared a pizza—Shelby still doesn't cook—and I'm just a little jealous of Burke's life.

He might have lost his sight, but he gained a beauty I once had, that I long for again.

That might be lost to me forever.

I find the Porsche—it's already unlocked from the fob I carry in my pocket, and as I climb in, Queen pummels the sound system with "We Will Rock You."

No, I'm not returning these wheels anytime soon.

I pull out, my thoughts threading back to our late night conversation about Eve. We reconstructed a possible timeline—one that started the moment Shelby called her to the hospital after my shoulder was dislocated during the pursuit of a perp named Bryce Mattson. Eve showed up and stayed with me while my shoulder was reset and that was where Shelby found us and recruited me to relay the bad news of Mattson's death to his parents.

Eve left me, presumably headed back to work.

Sometime in the next two hours, she called me.

I called her back, twice. Got her voice mail both times.

Then I went to her house to wait for her, built a fire, and fell asleep on the sofa. Eve was abducted and murdered during that three-hour period between the time she left me to the moment where I called Booker to tell him I didn't want the watch anymore,

Because I'd fixed it all. I had a happy ending waiting for me on this side.

Booker showed up on Eve's doorstep moments later with the news that she'd gone missing. And then my time was up.

Remember what I said about hope?

Shelby, Burke and I ran through the crime timeline over and again, and two things hang in my mind.

Why did Eve park a few blocks away, in front of a church instead of in the lot outside police HQ?

And, why is this personal? What did I do to tick off the Jackson killer? Sure, I dogged him for twenty-some years, but that's in the future. The future is where he'll find Eve and kill her for the first time. The future is also where we'll discover he's buried five of his victims in the backyard of my childhood home.

But this past is too young for him to have met me, to know me, my life, the people I love.

Too young for this to be a cat and mouse chase.

So, why Eve, *then?*

Worse, if this is personal, and I don't find the killer, Eve will be killed again, even if I save her from this death.

But all this is resting on the hope that Art can get the watch working. *Please.*

Whatever sunshine I carried with me from Florida is washed away with the rain and my dismal summations.

I'm back in my apartment, trying to figure out what a guy wears when he's the hired thug of a mobster when I get another text. I almost ignore it—yes, yes, Alexander, I know—but I notice it's not from our favorite mob boss, but Frankie.

I figured it out.

I press dial and she answers without a greeting. "Not on the phone."

Seriously? "You think I'm being bugged?"

"I think you need to see this. But, yes. I wouldn't put anything past you-know-who."

Probably I shouldn't, either. "Right. Okay, I'm coming over." I'm about to hang up when she interrupts me—

"I'm not at home."

My guess is that my appearance with the Porsche outside her house has her spooked. I don't blame her. I don't relish the idea of the Malakov brothers finding out I let her go.

"Are you at Booker's?"

I get a laugh. "Are you kidding me? No way. It's crazy over there. I'm at Zeke's."

I want to ask why it's crazy at Booker's one-and-a-half story craftsman bungalow near Lake Hiawatha—the house I probably wanted to emulate when we bought our own craftsman—but she hangs up.

I have no idea where Zeke lives, thank you. I grab a white T-shirt and pick up my phone. Find Zeke's name and press dial.

Voice mail.

I hang up.

Then I try my trick I did in the Porsche, pulling up recently visited locations on my phone.

Apparently, I still like the Thai place down the street. And I now know all of Alexander's places of operation. Besides Turbo, he—meaning me—hangs out a lot at Quincy's downtown, my old gym turned fight club. Of course, because of my surveillance of my old home, that's listed, along with the cemetery at Groveland, where Eve is laid to rest and where Booker found me two days ago, clutching the earth as my world careened out of control.

But one familiar location has me blinking.

Eve's place on Webster Avenue, the cute cottage that she owned before we were married, the one she renovated from top to bottom.

The place I last saw her.

Someone else lives there, someone I've visited more than once.

Fate is like that—it recycles people and places and events.

I pocket the phone and take a chance. Sorry, Alex, you're not getting the Porsche back anytime soon.

The rain has stopped and the sun has made an appearance, so I put the top down and crank up Foreigner's "Feels Like the First Time," as I drive the familiar route to Eve's place.

A crazy nostalgia sweeps through me at the sight of Eve's house, as if, in a way, it contains pieces of her soul. It hasn't updated since my last visit twenty-three years ago. The house needs a new paint job to refresh the white, and the roof could use reshingling.

But the lawn had been recently cut, and the hosta that Eve planted so many years ago are massive clumps along the front porch.

I pull up to the curb and get out.

The door opens before I can leave the sidewalk. "Seriously? What is it with you and parking that car like a siren in front of everyone's house?"

Frankie stands on the porch.

See, I can still trust my hunches.

"Sorry. You want me to put it in the garage? Or a couple blocks away?"

"Just get inside." She holds the door open and looks down the street, both ways.

"You okay?" I say as I climb the porch steps.

"Fine. Have you heard from Zeke?" She lets me inside and closes the door. Locks it.

My gaze goes to the stairway where I sat one night, shaken that I'd nearly gotten Danny Mulligan, Eve's father, killed.

Right here, in this entry way, I proposed to Eve.

"Inspector?"

I look at Frankie. She's got her dark hair pulled back, wears a pair of thick black glasses, a T-shirt with the arms cut off and joggers.

She looks like she might have been up all night.

"I'm fine. Just…Déjà vu."

"Yeah, well, if you're remembering the case that jump started your career, then yes."

The case that— "Frankie, have you been reading *The Last Year*?"

"The infamous memoir of Inspector Rembrandt Stone?" She leads me through the house toward the dining room. "It's dog-eared."

Great. I wrote the book my rookie year as an investigator, and miraculously it not only got published but in an outlier of fate, hit the New York Times best-seller list.

I notice that the house is furnished with a worn leather sofa, a couple club chairs and a huge flat-screen television over the fireplace. A bachelor pad in serious need of a female touch.

Frankie goes over to a dark-wood dining table and sits down in front of her computer.

The room is still painted Powell Buff, a hue I suggested, and my throat is thick as I pull up a chair next to her. "The case that jump started my career was a missing four-year-old from Minnehaha Park." Even as I say it, bells are dinging in the back of my head. I pause to see if anything emerges, but they go silent.

"Sorry," Frankie says, "You're right. I'm thinking of the case my father says was your first big victory, the coffee shop bombings."

I'd hardly count those as a victory. Two coffee shops blew up, at the hands of an immigrant soccer player from Columbia named Ramses Vega.

His mother was the Minneapolis mayor in my last lifetime. We had a few go-rounds—I wasn't her favorite dog in the pack, but as interim chief of police, we had to work together.

I pity the person who's on her radar today.

But, still, I did stop the last bombing, and sent Ramses to prison for a couple decades.

"Are you saying the Russians are planning a bombing of coffee shops?"

"Not quite that on the nose, but…" She turns her computer screen toward me. "Embedded in Malakov's files, I found this. It's a diagram—"

"Of a suitcase bomb," I say quietly.

She's right. I recognize the mechanisms, the elements. The

potential. "It's the same design as the coffee shop bombings, twenty-three years ago."

She glances at me. "It's a little more elegant. I studied that case. This is smaller, and there's one main difference…" She points to a small circle on the outside of the box. "This is not a dirty bomb. It's a bio bomb."

"A bio bomb?"

"As in biological weapon. When it's activated, it releases a neuro gas that paralyzes everyone in a hundred-yard radius. It's not about destruction—it's about annihilation."

"It just hurts people, not places." Like a place Malakov would like to acquire in his territorial grab. "What kind of gas?"

"Have you heard of Botulinum toxin?"

"Botulism, as in the food poisoning?"

"Yes. And you've heard of Botox, right?"

"Sure."

"Tiny, minuscule doses of botulinum toxin are used in cosmetic shots. It's a paralytic. But in its pure form, it one of the fastest acting neurotoxins, and the most lethal. A single gram of pure crystalline toxin could kill a million people if it was evenly dispersed and inhaled. Up until now, however, a method of distribution hasn't been developed. It needs to be bound to an ultrafine powder to be disseminated." She taps her screen. "I think the Brotherhood has figured it out."

Oh man. And I thought I had problems before…

"In liquid form, it's odorless and colorless, but it could be released in a vaporous form in a closed room and…"

"And you think this is what the Brotherhood is planning?"

"Yes. Although, I don't know when, or how."

You know what I'm thinking. If only the watch worked, I could go back in time and prevent all this, too.

And stop the shooting—I know, I know what you're thinking. I can't stop every crime, save everyone. I get that. But we're talking a *bio-bomb*, people.

But maybe you're right. I've already screwed up so much. And because of it, now I've *broken* the watch. I need to stop thinking I can simply hit rewind to solve my problems.

We'll just have to stop it the old-fashioned way.

"Excellent work, Frankie. I'll see what I can find out. Maybe we simply follow Alexander to the source. Can you put a trace on his phone?"

She looks at me like I'm a kindergartner. "If you can get me close enough to it, again. I just need to grab the signal, download software onto the device, and we can monitor all his movements."

Which means I probably need to return the Porsche.

Shoot.

"Good work, Frankie." I get up.

She puts a hand on my arm. "If you see Zeke, can you, um…" She makes a face. "I'm worried. He didn't come home last night, and…" She shrugs. "I know he can't always check in, but something doesn't feel right."

I touch her hand. I'm about to reassure her that everything's okay, that I was undercover for years while I was dating Eve, back in our original, real life, and sometimes she went for weeks without hearing from me.

For her safety, and mine.

But maybe Zeke isn't as big of a jerk as I am.

"I'll find him, Frankie."

She nods, worry in her eyes. "Take this." She hands me what looks like a hard drive. "It's programmed to upload the software when it finds his signal. It'll take about sixty seconds, and you'll need to be no more than three feet away."

"Got it."

She nods again. "Just… be careful, okay."

I give a quick smile and make my way to the Porsche. I'm also starting to get a bad feeling.

Overhead, the sky is darkening again, so I put up the top. *Minnehaha Park.* The name is still dinging in the back of my head, and it's only as I pull away, to Police's "Every Breath You Take," that I figure it out.

It's where Eve's body was found.

My own breath is caught as I slow and sit at the stop sign, the realization running through me.

The killer read my memoir. Studied it. He knew my history.

He has been playing a game from the *very beginning.*

My brain is churning as I take Hennepin all the way to Washington, winding my way to Quincy's.

It can't be someone I arrested—I worked homicide. Everyone we put behind bars was still serving time when Jackson made his first kill in the fall of '97.

And because of the marked up twenty, I know, right down to my bones, that it's the Jackson killer who took Eve.

I pull up outside Quincy's just as the sky opens up again, this time accompanied by thunder and lightning and a downpour that turns my T-shirt transparent by the time I get inside.

The building is dark, but I see light in the back, in the free weight area and I hear voices, the sounds of guys working out, at the far end of the gym. Thuds of a heavy bag, and grunting.

I swing my—Alexander's—keys around my finger as I head toward the back, adding a hint of swagger, trying to fit back into the skin of Staz.

The sooner we track down the Brotherhood's plan, the sooner I put Alexander away and extricate myself from this life.

But hopefully, before that, Art comes to my rescue.

More sounds, and this time I hear a groan that doesn't sound like it comes from someone pushing steel.

I pass the fight square and walk through the open doors to the back.

And stop, my heart a fist.

Zeke is hanging from the pull-up bar by his wrists, his feet barely touching the ground.

And, he's bleeding. From the nose, the mouth, his eyes swollen, groaning from deep inside his body.

Vita is standing away from him, breathing hard. Another man is standing beside him, also bloody.

Apparently it takes two able bodied men to beat up a defenseless guy.

They look at me, and I don't care as I shake my head.

The other man I've seen before, I know it. He has reddish brown hair, is in his early forties, and has a tattoo of a snake around his neck. Scars mark his face, old fight wounds, maybe, and he looks at me like we're ancient enemies.

Oh goodie, another work friend.

Alexander is sitting on the seat of a bench press, drinking a cup of coffee from the nearby CityPerk. And apparently, it's a family affair because a man who looks eerily like him stands, arms folded, holding up the brick wall and watching.

Boris.

"What's going on?" I say, my voice easy.

Zeke doesn't look at me, but Vita glances over, and smiles. "Sorry we got started without you."

Have I mentioned how I hate my life?

I say nothing, but look at Alexander. He lifts a shoulder and gestures to Zeke with his coffee. "We found our mole."

CHAPTER 8

In the past three lifetimes, Zeke has been like a son to the Rembrandt who lived those lives.

And, memory leakage means that the longer I stay, the more he's like a son to me too.

He looks rough, is half conscious, and if he hasn't talked yet, he will. It's only a matter of time before self-preservation wins.

"The mole?" I ask, not sure what sort of history this conversation has.

"I thought maybe that girl getting into my office might be an inside job," Alexander says.

The gig is up, and I know it. There's no way Zeke and I are both walking out of here with our covers intact. It's now or never.

If I remember Frankie's instructions correctly, I need to be within three feet of Alexander's phone for the device in my pocket to work, and since he seems the type to never be without it, I step closer to him, my brain starting an internal stop watch.

I have sixty seconds to download this program, keep Vita from killing Zeke, and figure out how to save my fellow mole.

Ready, go.

"How do you know this is our mole?"

"We saw him on the security camera," Boris says. He has more of an accent than Alexander, and I hope he doesn't start talking Russian because then we're really in trouble. He's overweight, wearing jogging pants and a T-shirt, and his years in the clink are etched on his face, in scars and fury. "We saw him kiss her, right after the cops came in. She left with him."

"He was probably the one who called them," Alexander says. He's the refined, high-end version of gangster in suit pants and dress shirt. He's showered, and sits like he's in a board room, listening to the pros and cons of a new venture.

Kissing on camera, in a gangsters' den, as the police were closing in and all hell was about to break loose. Yeah, that sounded like Zeke. Genius.

"She got away from you," Vita says. He's shorter than me, and a nick in his knuckles tells me that maybe Zeke put up a fight. I slowly clench my fist. I'd really like to pick up where Zeke left off.

"Maybe you're in it with him," Boris says.

I give him a look and buy some time with a rude gesture. Thirty more seconds.

The other guy, the redhead, has walked over to where he's stashed his towel. He picks it up and wipes his forehead like he's put in a few rounds.

Poor Zeke is bound to the pull-up bar with zip tie cuffs.

Easy enough.

"What's he after?" I say of Zeke, frowning, as if there's nothing nefarious for the Brotherhood to hide.

Alexander lifts a shoulder. "He's a cop."

"They must have gotten wind of what's about to go down." Boris says, and picks at his teeth. They're gold, like his brother.

I'm running out of stall tactics. Ten seconds.

"They're too late." Alexander sneers, taking a sip of his coffee. He looks at me. "Everything's already in play. By tomorrow we're going to own this city. End him."

I glance at Vita, who looks disappointed. But, apparently I have only one job, so I smile at him. "Thanks for warming him up for me."

Vita narrows his eyes, but moves away from Zeke as I pick up a bar used for lifting free weights.

The redhead sits down on a leg press bench. I calculate how long it will take for him to extricate himself and reach me.

I think I can do this.

Time's up. Software uploaded.

I look at Vita. "Clearly you don't know what you're doing."

Let me pause here to say that I've been working out at Quincy's for twenty-five years. I know this place. I know the smells, the nooks and crannies, the sounds the building makes when it's cold.

I know where the owner kept the keys, and I have one very clear memory of the time some wise guy tossed a bottle of water to a buddy across the room and managed to take out a sprinkler.

We couldn't use the weight room for two weeks.

I'm counting on that memory now as I raise the bar and step up to Zeke. *Too late. Everything's already in play.* The words are zinging around in the back of my head as I mentally block out the men behind me. If everything's already in play, then either I have no memory of it...

Or I'm already out of the loop. Which means, and this is a very real possibility...they don't trust me. I saw the way Boris looked at me, didn't you?

They could very well have a gun pointed at my kidneys right now.

"Sorry, pal. We don't like cops," I say.

Then I turn, and like one of my baseball heroes, Kirby Puckett, I swing hard.

I connect with Vita for a homer, and he goes down like a rock. Alexander is too stunned to move, but Boris shouts, heading toward me.

The sprinkler above me is next, and it's another direct hit.

The other two sprinklers in the room react in a second, and it rains, drenching the room.

Now Alexander hits his feet, shouting, in Russian. He's dropped his coffee—

And then he's down, another victim of my Kirby swing.

My rampage is over though, because the redhead has reached me. He's too close for the bar, so I turn and level him with a punch, and he stumbles back.

Boris takes me down in a blinding tackle at the waist. I skid across the floor, roll and barely catch his knife hand on its way toward my chest.

Sheesh, the man is huge, and we're rolling around on the floor in puddles of water. Sirens have sounded, too, and I'm sure, just like last time, the alarm system is connected with the local fire department.

We have less than five minutes.

Sparks shoot from the electrical system.

I'm either going to fry, or bleed to death.

I pick C, none of the above. Rolling, I get my knee into fat Boris' soft places—there's no honor in desperation—and he howls, spits out Russian and it's enough for me to untangle myself.

I grab the knife, and bounce back.

Redhead is there.

I employ an old Irish mafia trick—a slash across his forehead, above his eyebrows.

He goes blind with the blood and falls to his knees.

I can almost hear Eve, back in my head. *It's just a flesh wound.* Words to our daughter when she nicked her forehead at the park. I was more freaked out than she was as we drove to the hospital, her teddy bear clutched to her chest, Eve pressing a towel to her head.

An inopportune memory, because it has the power to paralyze me—

But right then, and just like I'd hoped, the lights go off.

Nothing but pitch blackness back here, in the windowless weight room.

Like I said, I *know* this place. Three steps and I'm at the pull up bar. I find Zeke's hands and slice the zip ties. He falls like a side of beef into my arms.

There's also no finesse in desperation, and while Boris curses in Russian, I flip Zeke over my shoulder.

I run with a stiff arm and manage to hit Boris on my way out. I'm guessing Redhead is still down for the count, bleeding into his eyes.

The barest dent of light at the front of the building, despite the storm, beckons, and I'm practically on fire as I lumber toward the door.

No, really, I almost *am* burning because the sparks from the overhead lights have fallen into a nearby bin of towels and mats and ignited. The place clouds with smoke as flames brighten around me.

Red lights smudge the graying air as Zeke and I break free of the building. An engine has pulled up in front, and I spot a man in turnout gear climbing out of the front cab. Coughing, I tell him there are four more people inside.

But it's occurred to me, should the Malakov brothers perish in this fire, that might end a few of our problems.

Or, if things are already in play, maybe it wouldn't matter.

I can't unravel it now—Zeke needs a hospital stat. My new Porsche responds like we were made for each other as I approach, unlocking her doors for me. I pile Zeke into the front seat as more engines arrive.

I dial Frankie as I punch it down Washington toward Hennepin County Medical Center. "Found him," I say without greeting. "Meet me at HCMC."

Then I hang up before she can ask me more questions.

Behind me, smoke rises into the grimy afternoon, the rain still pinging down on my windshield.

That's one way to burn your cover, I guess.

C'mon, that was funny. ,

Fine. But, for one, I'm relieved not to be Staz the Thug anymore. However, I just destroyed twenty years of hard-earned cover and the Rembrandt whose history I just dismantled might want a go at me. But I wasn't going to let Zeke die.

I pull up in the emergency entrance, get out, whip around to Zeke's side of the car and help him to his feet. He groans and opens his eyes.

"Hey buddy," I say.

He's looking up at me, as if he doesn't know me. Then, "Staz?"

Oh boy. "It's over, buddy. You're safe."

He's just staring at me. And then his eyes close again.

"Help! I could use a little help over here!" I don't know what kind of internal injuries he might have sustained, but I do see bruising on his torso as I drag up his shirt. I duck and pull him over my shoulder again and by this time an orderly arrives with a wheelchair.

Good enough. I dump him into it. "He's been beaten," I say, as if it isn't obvious.

The man takes him back to the emergency area, a large room cordoned off by hanging curtains. They roll him into a bay and another orderly helps lift him onto an examination table.

A doctor comes over, and leans it back, checking for a pulse, then asks for oxygen. He turns, and looks at me, something of accusation in his eyes.

I guess I must look a type. "I didn't do this."

His mouth purses.

"Don't let him die," I say, then, a little edge to my voice, because if that's what he thinks, I'll own it.

He pulls the curtain.

I'm left standing in the middle of the hallway, the antiseptic, cottony smells of a hospital finding me, dragging me back to the past.

To Eve, in my arms, for the last time.

"Is that a yes, then, to my question?"

"You knew I was going to say yes, just admit it."

Oh, wow, I need to sit down.

I find a chair in the lobby just as Frankie storms into the ER lobby. She's wearing a dress and heels, her hair up, like she's come from a party.

"Frankie!"

She spots me and runs over. I stand up and am a little undone when she wraps her arms around me. "Thank you, Rembrandt. Thank you."

"Don't thank me yet," I say, and put her away, holding her arms. "He's pretty badly beaten up."

She's shaking. "How did they find out?"

I don't want to tell her. So, yes, I lie. "You know…they just did."

She considers me, and deep down, I think she knows. But she

just nods. "Can I see him?"

"Yes." You know that doc isn't standing in my way. But, just in case something terrible is happening in there, I ask her to stay put while I do some reconnaissance.

I head back into the ER, and the curtain is still closed, but I open it and find the doc doing some ad hoc surgery. He's inserted a line into Zeke's chest, and blood is draining from it.

But Zeke is breathing.

Doc stares at me. I must look concerned because he relents and nods. "We need to get him into the OR."

"His girlfriend is here."

"Two minutes," he says and I scoot out to get Frankie.

She practically sprints back, and I'll just get in the way, so I'm standing, awkwardly in the waiting room when Danny Mulligan, Eve's father walks in.

He's lean, wears a fierceness in his expression that should turn the blood of Boris Malakov to ice.

I stand there, wanting to sort of blend into the beige walls when he spots me.

It takes a second, and in that space of time, I'm trying to get a fix on our relationship.

Does he think it's because of me that his daughter was murdered? That I loved her more than breath in my body? Does he know I'll do anything to get her back?

"Rembrandt." And then he walks over to me, purposefully and presses his hand into mine. "You're okay. We were worried when we couldn't find you, after the Malakov's gym burned down."

"I am, sir." And don't mind me, but I suddenly feel twenty-eight, still wishing the man liked me. Then I fix my gaze on his eyes and think maybe he does.

"Alexander Malakov is in custody, with charges of attempted

murder of a police officer."

"And Boris?"

"No sign of him. But we picked up one of their associates. I'm assuming the artwork is yours?"

The redhead.

Although, Vita and Boris are still at large. "I blew my cover."

He steps back, considers me. "Eve would be proud of you."

I stare at him, my chest tight. Then he nods, and his own eyes are misty.

"Chief," Frankie says as she comes out of the ER area. "What are you doing here?"

Chief? But maybe that's right, although the man is long past retirement.

"I came to check on Zeke. How's our boy?"

"He's going into surgery to stop internal bleeding," she says. She looks at me. "Rembrandt saved his life."

Aw, shoot. She has a little hero worship in her eyes. Her voice cuts low, then, "Did you find out where…" And she raises an eyebrow, clearly not willing to say the word, bomb, in public.

"No. But according to Alexander, it's already in play."

She glances at Danny. He nods. "Okay. We'll have a go at him and see what we can find out." He turns to me. "You, get that cut looked at."

I look down and see that my shirt is red, a nick from Boris' knife in my shoulder.

"It's just a flesh wound," I say, aching suddenly for Eve.

Danny smiles. "You've had worse." He winks, starts for the door.

"I'm keeping the Porsche," I shout after him.

CHAPTER 9

Something in my gut—and no, it's not the pepperoni Hot Pocket I ate around midnight—tells me this isn't over.

Okay, the words, "everything's already in play," are a glaring clue, but it's *more* than that.

It's like time is trying to tell me something, and the answer to all this is sitting in the back of my brain, already there, waiting, but refusing to be dislodged.

Or maybe I'm just exhausted.

The sun has found its way through the woven shade of Zeke's hospital room. I'm achy, and crabby and no amount of coffee is going to clear the sense of doom that has invaded my cells over the past twelve hours.

Somewhere, out in the city, there's a bomb. And I haven't a clue where it might be.

I cannot escape the sense that I dropped the ball, despite my instinct to save Zeke.

"Rembrandt? What are you still doing here?"

The voice turns me and Frankie walks into the room.

She left last night, not long after Zeke woke up, briefly,

recognized her and then slipped back into unconsciousness. I told her I'd stick around and keep an eye on him.

Not just so I could question him, but again, because of that clench in my gut that this isn't over. I can't dismiss the idea that Boris or Vita, who also vanished after the fire, might show up and finish what they started.

Frankie is again wearing a dress, dark blue and lacy, and heels. I frown at her. "You look nice."

"Thanks," she says, and checks her watch. Looks at me. "I guess you have time."

I know you're asking—for what? Me too. But Frankie doesn't know I'm not really me, and I don't want to act like I've been hit in the head, so I just nod.

At the moment, there is nothing more important than waiting for Zeke to wake up to ask him what he knows, so yeah, Frankie's right, I do have all the time in the world.

She pulls up a chair next to him. Puts her hand on his arm. "Zeke? Honey?"

He groans. Maybe I should have tried that trick. His eyes open and it takes a second, but he finds her face.

Smiles.

I remember looking like that, a few times, when Eve smiled down at me. Like my world started and stopped on her beautiful face.

I turn away and open the shade as they talk, as she kisses him.

The sun is up, shining gold on the skyline. I'd guess it's about mid-morning.

"I'll be back later," I hear Frankie say.

I look at Zeke, back to her. She's staring at me. "I know we just met, really, but…thank you, Rembrandt, for everything. I hope that…well, don't be late, okay?"

Right. "I wouldn't think of it."

She gives me a smile, then leaves.

I turn back toward Zeke and walk over to him. "How you feeling?"

He groans. "Like I got run over by a buffalo."

"Yeah, well you look like it. You can thank Vita," He's reaching for the bed remote and I grab it and hand it to him. He raises the bed to a sitting position, wincing a little before it stops and he sighs, adjusting to his pain.

"Apparently, I should be thanking you."

I sit down in the chair Frankie just vacated. "Naw. Right place, right time."

And funny, but the words hit me. That's my story. Right place, right time. Just maybe not the right life.

No, my life is full of true lies, that I tell just to keep up.

"Zeke," I lean forward. "The Brotherhood is cooking up a plan to set up a biological bomb somewhere. Do you have any idea where that might be?"

He makes a face. "Sorry. No. That's why I went back to Quincy's…I thought maybe I could wheedle it out of Vita, or maybe Daggert—he loves to run his mouth. But…they were waiting for me."

Daggert. I *know* that name.

A knock comes at the door and I sit back as a nurse comes into take Zeke's vitals. She's not there long when the ER doc from last night arrives to check on Zeke. "Good thing your friend brought you in when he did."

Yeah, yeah, I'm a hero. Maybe someone should point out that I'm the one that got Zeke into this mess in the first place, or at least the Rem from this timeline had.

The doc is leaving when, with another knock, a familiar face comes into the room.

I go cold.

"Hey, Zeke. I was here doing some rounds when I heard you were here. I thought I'd duck in and see how you are."

I'm staring at Gene Latsky, my old physical therapist. He looks the same as last time I left him, except he's twenty-three years older, with thinning blond hair, tall, a tiny paunch. He's wearing a black HCMC pullover with an ID badge around his neck, a pair of jeans and tennis shoes.

And a sleeve. A full tattoo sleeve I know I would have noticed before. My gaze is glued to it when he sees me. "Rembrandt Stone? Is that you?" He holds out his hand. "I haven't seen you in…what, maybe twenty years."

I stand. "Gene. How are you?"

He smiles at me. "I'm good." He steps back. "Wow, I didn't realize you were still on the job."

I can see the headlines rolling through his eyes, the ones that framed me for Burke's murder.

"Things aren't always as they seem," I say.

"Indeed," he wears an enigmatic look.

And you know I'm taking a good look at him, testing him against my gut to see if he's a man who could kill thirty-eight women, murder my daughter and strangle my wife. He has big hands.

"Well, I'm glad to hear you're still around and chasing down bad guys. And clearly Zeke is in good hands." He turns to leave, but I can't quite let him go.

"Nice sleeve," I say.

He stops, looks at his arm. "Thanks."

"I didn't know you had a tattoo."

"Aw, old war injury. Decided I needed a little art so I didn't scare my patients."

I don't remember the injury. "I didn't know you were in the war."

"Long time ago, when I was just a kid. First Infantry."

The Big Red One. My heart gives a bang in my chest.

The Jackson killer had a tattoo, one that we chased down to Leo. Who served in the Big Red One.

"By the way, Rem…I'm so sorry about Eve." Gene's voice is warm, his eyes almost compassionate. "Isn't today the anniversary of her death?"

"Yes," I say, a little nonplussed that he'd remember that. "Thanks. It's good of you to think of her."

He shakes his head. "I'll never forget that night. I'd just seen you both, and then…just like that she was gone. So tragic."

I had forgotten that we'd seen him that night, caught in the haze of Mattson and Leo's deaths. Gene had just reset my shoulder. He'd left, and I pulled Eve close.

She probably thought I was going to kiss her. Instead, being the romantic I am, I said, *"I'd like you to track down a guy named Gio Rossi. See if he died in Desert Storm. He would have been a member of the First Infantry Division."*

"The Big Red One. The same division at Fitzgerald?"

"They served together. But more than that, they were half-brothers."

I remember looking out into the hallway, where Gene had left, and saying that I thought maybe I'd seen a ghost.

The memory still roots a shiver through me.

It was the first time I suggested, aloud, that Fitzgerald might be innocent. After all, he kept saying Johnny was the killer. But I'd pinned him to the crimes and even the one in the past through the Toronado his stepfather, Nick Latsky, drove.

Nick, not-a-relation-to-Gene Latsky, according to Gene. I

even mentioned the weird coincidence of the last name to Eve.

She shrugged it off. *"It's a common last name. Polish, I think. I'm sure we could find two hundred Latskys in the St. Paul phone book."*

So, I did too. After all, I'd taken Leo Fitzgerald out of the picture.

I thought I'd saved us all.

Now, I have the craziest, inexplicable urge to go for Gene's throat, which makes no sense. He was Eve's friend. He helped her mother get mobility back after being shot.

And me—he set my shoulder, and before that helped me get back in action after a stabbing.

Just calm down, Stone. "Yes. Very tragic," I say without emotion. "And we haven't caught her killer yet. But there's no statute of limitations on murder. I'll get him. It's just a matter of time." I level my gaze at him.

"I'm sure you will," he says, still wearing the compassion. He looks at Zeke. "Get better."

Then he's gone, and I'm sweating.

It can't be him, can it?

"Rem?"

"I'm okay." I turn to Zeke. "Except, can you please tell me what I'm late for?"

He stares at me, and then his eyes widen. "Oh no. Booker's *wedding.*"

"His *what?*"

Before he can answer, my phone rings. I swipe it out of my pocket.

Art. Saving my life, I hope. "What do you have for me?"

"Not good news."

I close my eyes, run my hand across my forehead. "Just tell me."

"Well, there's nothing physical on the watch causing the gears to freeze. They haven't been damaged in any way, and according to my examination, it looks like they *should* work."

"Did you try turning the dial?"

"It still doesn't spin. But I've been thinking about our conversation regarding the intent of the watch. Is it possible that instead of solving a cold case, you *created* one?"

Oh, I knew it. "Booker thought the same thing. But we can't find a cold case in my history—"

"Maybe the case belonged to someone else. Like your partner?"

"Shelby?"

He pauses. "I thought you had a male partner."

"Right. Andrew Burke."

I've wandered out into the hallway for our call, not wanting Zeke to hear words like *time travel*. Because, well, you get it. "If it wasn't my case, could I still use it to, um," A nurse has walked by, so I cut my voice low. "Travel?"

"Maybe, because he was your partner. Or maybe, you could get the case assigned to you. I'm not exactly sure how this works."

For a time travel guide, he isn't exactly five star. Still, Art is all I have.

I watch the nurse walk down the hallway. She stops in front of a room guarded by a uniform, and I follow her down, my hunches suddenly firing, as if my collision with Gene has loosed something.

"So, if I found the new case, the one I somehow unsolved, and got it assigned to me...and had the watch..."

I've stopped outside the room. The nurse is coming out and I peek inside.

The redheaded thug is on the bed, his head bandaged where I drew a line with Boris' blade. Jimmy Daggert, Danny called him.

"In theory," Art says, "but that would mean figuring out how you could have possibly interfered enough to cause a case to go cold. And then, of course, when? It might be nowhere near the time of your wife's death. Remember a thousand tiny choices..."

As the door soft closes, I catch a glimpse, again of the snake tattoo that rings Daggert's neck.

From a distance, it looks like a rope.

Everything inside me seizes. Wow, I am a certifiable idiot. "I need the watch, Art."

I cast a grim smile at the uniform and keep walking, wondering if anyone else can hear the terrible thunder of my pulse.

"Of course. But why?"

"I figured it out." I can barely breathe as I hit the elevator button. "I'm coming for the watch."

"I'm in...well, I'm here, Rembrandt. I'm at city hall."

The door dings, and I step in. "Why are you at city hall?"

But the reception cuts out as the doors close.

"Art?"

The call is dropped.

No problem, because the cold case files are housed in basement of city hall, in the police department wing.

Eve, I'm on my way.

I still have the Porsche, and I find it in the lot and climb in. 38 Special is singing, "If I'd Been the One," and I'm trying to keep it under thirty as I drive through the city.

James Daggert.

The name of Bryce Mattson's cousin. You remember Bryce, right? The shooter from Jin's Liquors who died at the monster truck rally.

C'mon, it's a hard image to forget.

But maybe you don't remember the other connection.

Jimmy Daggert is also Bianca Potter's boyfriend. Poor Bianca, the woman who died outside The 400 Bar, at the hands of said boyfriend, a connection that should have been made when her car was searched. If it *had* been searched, then Burke would have found a restraining order, filled out and shoved into her glove compartment.

With the restraining order as probable cause, a warrant would have been issued, Jimmy arrested, and his DNA matched to the cigarette butts found at the scene.

Jimmy Daggert should have gone down for Bianca Potter's murder twenty-three years ago.

I know. You're banging your hand on your head, too. I'm wracking my mind to remember if I reminded Burke to search Bianca's car. But probably not—it was sitting in impound after I tracked down Bryce at the auto shop where he nicked it to use for the liquor store robbery.

In which Daggert was his accomplice.

I did this. I impounded Bianca's car as evidence and iced the case.

Bam.

I pull up in the ramp across the street from police HQ, lock my Porsche and head inside.

I've stopped taking for granted the things that outlive us, those buildings that pass from generation to generation, storing within their walls the history that binds us together. Minneapolis City Hall is such a building. Built in 1888, it's made of rose granite and rises five stories above the city, encompasses an entire city block and houses both the city police department and the county offices. In the center of the building, under a five-story rotunda, is a sculpture of Neptune, the father of the sea.

Sometimes, events are held in the massive lobby, and now,

music filters down the marble hallway as I walk through the back entrance toward the Minneapolis Police Department.

I'm taking a chance that the cold case will be housed here, and not at the precinct office down by the river.

Security has tightened since I was here last, and I'm stopped by a walk-through scanner and a uniform before I can enter the police wing.

He gives me a look and I know what he sees. A rumpled, probably grimy guy wearing last night's clothes, a thick shadow of whiskers on his jaw and fading bruises from the brawl a few nights back. I might even smell like smoke.

I probably should have showered before arriving.

I raise my hands. "I'm a cop," I say to the young buck, who, for me, is anyone under the age of forty.

"I'm going to need ID," he says, and of course, I'm a badge short. I'm sizing him up, debating, when I hear a voice behind me.

"Let him through."

I turn, and spot Danny Mulligan heading toward us. He's wearing a suit and tie, looking clean shaven and official.

The officer buzzes us both through. Danny is looking me up and down. Raises an eyebrow. "Really?"

I haven't a clue what he's talking about. "I need to pick up a file."

He checks his watch. "You have about ten minutes before the bride walks down the aisle."

Oh. He's talking about the *wedding*. I do quick math.

"The wedding is *here*? In the rotunda?"

"Okay, I get you not receiving an official invitation, but certainly you planned on at least sneaking in the back?"

I nod quickly, because, after all, it is Booker's wedding. "Yeah. But not staying. Boris Malakov is still out there and—"

He holds up his hand. "I get it. What file are you after?"

I know it's not a casual question. "Not Eve's, if that's what you're wondering."

His mouth makes a tight line. "Not a day goes by that we don't think about Eve. Or want her case solved. But I saw what it did to you before, and I just…I don't want you to go down that road again." He puts his hand on my shoulder, like he might be my father.

Huh.

"It's a different case. Bianca Potter."

He frowns, and I see him cataloging his past cases. He was there, too, with Burke, investigating her murder.

"Bartender killed outside a Minneapolis night club. We got DNA, but never got a match to it," he says, proving his investigative mind is still on the job.

"I think I know who we overlooked," I say as we reach the elevator in the department lobby. "She had a boyfriend we never checked out."

Danny sticks his hands into his pockets. "It was a difficult time. I'm sure I missed things, and not just on this case." The elevator is descending from an upper floor. "But what made you think of it?"

I'm tired of lying, so I tell a version of truth. "Jimmy Daggert—one of Malakov's men—was also one of my persons of interest in the shooting at Jin's Liquors. I'm not sure how he scooted under the radar." The elevator dings. "But seeing him triggered a memory. I need to check the files on Bianca. I'm almost positive he was her boyfriend."

Danny's eyebrows are raised. "Good memory."

"Things are starting to clear up." I step onto the elevator, pressing the basement button.

He frowns as the doors start to close, then sticks his hand in to stop them. "You'll need this." He reaches into his pocket and pulls out his badge. "I expect it back."

I take it as the doors close.

So, Booker is getting married. I can admit that surprises me, but I'm long past anything being earth-shattering.

The doors open into the catacombs of the basement storage. Long ago, everything was digitized, but for physical evidence, boxes are still kept, and with them the original case files.

A female officer is at the entrance. I check myself in with my name and Danny's badge number. She frowns at the discrepancy. "Inspector Stone, that isn't the right number."

"I know. I was at the wedding when Chief Mulligan sent me down to get the file." It's mostly true, if you keep a high-level view.

She eyes my clothes.

"I'm late," I say. "I was on a case."

Again, true.

She lets me through, and after a small description of the case, gives me a file number and location. "It's currently unassigned," she says as an update.

"Not any more. Assign it to me."

I find Bianca Potter's case bound in a thin brown accordion file. I take it to a table and open it.

Burke's handwriting is on it, but with his retirement, I can see why it fell off the radar into no man's land. No mention of Bianca's car, or any search of it, is in his notes.

I tuck it under my arm and head back upstairs.

The music is still playing, and as I leave the police wing, I'm drawn down the hall to the massive vestibule.

The place is decked out with round tables, gold chairs, and white and blue floral centerpieces. A buffet table is set up across the room, and in front of Neptune's sprawling body is a giant spray of white roses atop a carved pillar with bright lights glowing out of it.

Gloved waiters stand near the door, four of them, at attention. A small quartet is playing Pachelbel's Canon in D as guests stand below the massive stairway that spans the balconies bordering the area. I see mostly police uniforms—Danny is here, of course, but so are most of the deputy chiefs, the precinct commanders and inspectors, along with a large group of beat cops, also in uniform.

Booker is walking down one stairway, hatless, but also in uniform, his eyes on the bride, who is walking down the other stairway.

She's wearing a long gray-white dress with red embroidered flowers on the train, her hair up, and she's smiling.

I almost don't recognize her, and when I do, I am frozen.

Mariana Vega. The mayor, from a former lifetime, and mother of Ramses Vega, the bomber from my first rewrite of time.

How in the world ... When?

I'm scrolling back, through all my memories to see if, even once, Booker had a connection with her, and my surfing stops at the second bombing when he was interviewing her, the owner of one of the coffee shops.

How he nearly took my head off when I chased down her son.

Oh, Booker. What have you gotten into? But he's smiling like I've never seen him before, and so is she as they meet at the bottom and he takes her claw—er, hand.

I meant hand, *really*. Maybe she's different in this lifetime. People can change, right?

Frankie is standing at the front of the crowd, on the first step from the bottom, grinning.

So maybe this is a happy event. I'm going to attract attention in my current state, so I'm about to turn and leave when movement near the door, from the row of waiters catches my eye.

I still.

The gaze of Vita, my favorite tough, is pinned on me. We share a moment, not quite as beautiful as the one happening on the stairs opposite us.

Then he turns and flees. With the attention of the entire police force on Booker as he vows to love and cherish, no one sees Vita run.

But I do.

For a second, my instincts have my legs running to catch up.

Except. What is he doing here? And maybe you were already thinking this, but I've just realized it …

The bomb.

The event that will allow the Brotherhood to take over the city. I'm an idiot, and let's just say that if I'd just asked the right questions, maybe I would have seen this coming. But I'm here now, and I know, deep in my gut that the bomb is here.

It's like your first case.

Frankie's words ping inside me and my gaze goes to the coffee containers on the table.

But no, that would be too easy. I stand behind a column and think.

My eyes fall on the flower arrangement. And more importantly, the pillar. The one carved in a design to allow the free moment of, say, a gas. Or a toxin.

I tuck the file under my arm, duck my head and weave my way around the tables to the front of Neptune. Crouching in front of the flowers, I peer inside the pillar.

I wasn't lying about my hunches, although this one comes without the aid of time travel, and bingo! The canister wedged inside has a fist around my lungs.

Mariana is giving her vows as I lift down the floral arrangement, then find a latch to open the pedestal.

Twinkly lights are attached to the inside, and nestled in the middle of them is an egg-shaped container—what looks like an air atomizer—with slots at the top, and along the sides.

My hands are shaking as I remove it, and put it on the floor. A tiny neon timer flashes at the top.

I can only guess that it's been armed, probably by Vita as he fled the building. And your guess is as good as mine as to how much time I have.

My first instinct is to pick it up and run. Maybe hurtle it into a closet.

And then the light stops blinking.

No …

I'm waiting, of course, for the mist to release, to be paralyzed on the spot, and I hold my breath.

"Rembrandt?"

It's *Art.* I stare at him, then back to the egg.

He's holding out the watch.

And then it happens—a mist starts to emit from the egg, violent and loud and, true confession, I panic. I kick it away from me.

I'm still holding my breath, and I grab the watch.

I have two choices.

Run.

Grab the bomb and try and contain it or—

Okay, three choices.

I grab the watch, and wind the dial.

People are shouting, and Art's eyes are widening, and he starts to cough.

So do I, my chest tightening, seizing. I haven't escaped the gas.

It's over.

Then like an old friend, the rumble begins, the locomotive of time roaring to life.

CHAPTER 10

I close my eyes. And for the first time in ages, I hope.

I blink through the darkness, and in a moment, I'm standing in the middle of a dark alleyway, a frigid wind snaking into my wool jacket, and burning my ears.

My head is pounding, like someone took a bat to it, and it takes me a moment—a long moment, where I look at my black Jeep, at the sky overhead, thick with stars, and the movement of a twelve-foot tree in front of me, still shivering from a recent wound—until I realize where I am.

I'm standing behind my house, my future home, the one I bought with Eve and remodeled. And, I'm holding an axe.

Because I'm chopping down the someday-to-be diseased elm tree that will level our home—or would have, if fate and I hadn't derailed our life.

"Rem! Stop! What are you doing?"

The voice turns me, and I see Eve, my beautiful Eve, dressed in a thick parka, her hair pulled back, her eyes wide as she looks down the street as if on lookout.

Alive.

What am I doing? I look at the axe in my hand, and at the tree.

I've overlapped time, landing here at the moment of Bianca Potter's murder in Minneapolis. In two hours, Burke will hunt me down at the Gold Nugget, bring me to the crime scene, and the past will repeat itself.

Over the next twenty-four hours, Eve will be abducted and murdered.

No. Not this time.

I put the axe down and look at the tree.

Eve loves this tree.

Someday this tree will tower over our backyard, and Eve and I, looking for homes, will step out onto the deck of the in-need-of-remodel 1948 craftsman and she'll say, "Rem, look at that tree. It's beautiful."

And we will buy this house.

I can't believe I forgot that.

"You're not seriously cutting this tree down, are you?" She comes up to me, and I look at her.

She's alive. A little flummoxed, but alive.

"No," I say, and look at the axe. "No, I'm not."

And suddenly, I get it. A thousand tiny things...but I can't change them all, and most of all, every choice I make is a choice to change something else in the future. I don't know what it is, but I have learned that I can live with the past mistakes much easier than I can without the blessings of today.

"C'mon." She reaches out her hand, and I slide mine into it.

Nod.

She leads me to the Jeep, and I get inside, tossing the axe in the back and just, for a moment, breathe.

Fate—or maybe God, yes, I'm going there—has granted me a

do-over. One more ring around the watch face.

"I think you need to go to the ER and get checked for a concussion," she says, and I gingerly put my hand to my pounding head.

There's an egg-shaped welt there and now I remember Bryce Mattson taking a swipe at me with a ratchet this afternoon. "I'll be okay." I give her a pained grin. "Really."

"Then, let's go to my place. I don't want you falling asleep alone."

I know she doesn't mean it how it sounds. Still, I glance at her, because snippets of this recent past are returning to me, and I remember two distinct memories.

The first is nearly telling her that I time travel. Yes, I know, but I was as tired of the lies then as I am now.

The second is a very distinct, vibrant memory of what we started on my sofa in my apartment, and what prompted the sudden compelling urge to chop down a tree, which apparently is my substitute for a cold shower.

I meet her eyes in the darkness. "I'll go back to your place, Eve, but…" I swallow.

"Calm down, Rembrandt. I didn't invite you for a sleep over. I just want to keep an eye on you."

Yeah, well, I know us. Or the us from our first go-round.

And, I miss her so very much.

But I also don't want *her* to be alone, not until we have her killer in custody, so I nod, and put my Jeep into gear.

And I leave the tree to grow another twenty-three years. If it takes out the house, I'll be there, then, to stop it.

I hope.

We pull up to the familiar house on Webster. It's dark, and she leads me inside. "I'll get you some acetaminophen," she says and directs me to the sofa.

Instead, I get a fire going, hauling in wood from the back deck, leaving some logs inside the kitchen by the door so we don't have to make another trip.

I'm here for the night, and we both know it.

When she returns, she's changed clothes into sweatpants and a Henley.

"Hungry?" she asks.

"Ravenous," and it's true because I truly don't know the last time I ate.

"I'll put a frozen pizza in the oven."

I take out my ancient-slash-current cell phone, turn it off and put it on a side table. Sorry, Burke. I know he'll be looking for me, but I can't solve Bianca's cold case, not yet.

I wander to the kitchen where Eve is unwrapping the pizza. She looks so impossibly young, so impossibly beautiful, I blink away the images of her dead body in my mind's eye.

If I fail, she will forever be this Eve for me. Hazel-green eyes alight, glancing at me with something of a mischievous smile, and believing in me.

Oh, that's right. I had told her about my so-called hunches.

And, asked her to marry me, again.

She opens the oven, puts the pizza on the rack, and I come up behind her as she closes the door.

I see our reflections in the shiny glass. Eve, and behind her a much younger man, with mussed short dark hair, a little banged up, wearing a T-shirt and favoring a tender shoulder. But he's smiling as he wraps his arms around her from behind and presses a kiss to her neck.

He has so much hope. So much life yet to live.

I look at us. "We belong together, Eve. You and I, partners."

She smooths her hands down my arms and smiles at my reflection. Then she turns around to face me. "I was thinking about what you were saying about Florida, and moving there with me and…" She slides her hands up around my neck. "What if we stayed here?"

"And?"

"I'll marry you. Of course, I will." She presses her hand to my face. "But I also want to build my career. What did you say—become the head of my department?"

"I think I said award-winning, too." I lower my head and kiss her.

She tastes like coffee, and home and it's just us. She's my Eve, responding to my kiss, relaxing in my arms. I lean back against the counter and she steps between my legs and we are lost in each other.

I want to stay right here. With Eve. With the possibilities of an unwritten tomorrow.

With hope.

I think I might be crying because when she leans back, she presses her hand to my cheek, and there's wetness there. "Rem?" She frowns.

"I'm just tired," I say and try and laugh, but then it comes out pitiful and yeah, I'll admit it, I *am* crying.

What is wrong with me?

I push her away and press my hands to my face. "Sorry. I'm just…" But I can't stop the freakin' waterworks and I walk to the window, staring out into the darkness, not looking at the man in the reflection. "I'm just so scared."

I press my hand to my chest then, because I feel transparent, as if in a moment all this—me, her—could disappear.

Clearly, I'm a basket case.

Her hand touches my back, between my shoulder blades. "I'm

here, Rem. I'm not going anywhere."

My throat is thick, and I swallow and reach out my hand. And hers is there.

We stand, looking together into the darkness for a long moment. I take a breath. "Can I tell you something?"

She glances at me, meets my gaze, nods.

"It's going to sound crazy."

"Crazier than your magic hunches?"

I give her a half smile. "I'm afraid so."

She tilts her head. "I'm ready for crazy."

"I…I can travel in time."

She simply blinks at me. A hint of frown creases her face, then breaks free. "I'm listening."

I open my mouth, close it.

Stare at her. "How I love you, Eve Mulligan."

She smiles then. "I could have predicted that. Does that mean I can travel in time, too?"

"Funny." I pull her close, needing to hold onto her when I say the words. "I'm actually fifty-one years old, and we've been married for nearly ten years. We have a beautiful daughter named Ashley and live in that craftsman house with the tree I just tried to chop down."

She sighs. "I know. You told me."

I did, earlier, when I proposed, but I hold her away, my hands on her arms. "I told you because that's where I live. Or I lived."

She's just breathing, but I know her scientific mind is sorting through my words. Then, slowly, she takes my hands from her arms.

My chest rises and falls as she stands there. Then she takes my hand and leads me out of the kitchen, to the sofa.

Okay.

She licks her lips, captures the lower one. "Let's say, just for kicks, that I believe you. Tell me how."

Just for kicks. "It's this watch." I point to the timepiece, now ticking as if it never went rogue on us. "I got it from Booker, in the future. When I pair it with a cold case file, I can...well, sort of travel through time in my thoughts. I call it Chronothizing."

"Is that a word?"

"It is now. It's where you imagine yourself back in the past, imagine a different outcome, except I actually go back to my past, relive it and, well I've rewritten it."

"Oh—that's terrible."

She. Gets. It. Oh my, she gets it.

"You have no idea." I don't know where to start, but it occurs to me that if I want to save her, I'll need her help.

"The first time I went into the past, I caught the coffee shop bomber."

Her mouth opens. "Really? That was...um, you?"

"It's always me. Just sometimes, a different, older version of me."

She looks me over, up and down.

"Same body as the young me."

"But you're older, here." She presses her hand to my heart.

"And here." I touch my head. "I know things."

"About me. About *us*."

"Yes."

"Like my favorite coffee."

"Or what it will be. I might have planted that idea in your head."

She narrows her eyes. "And the ham salad sandwich from the deli."

"Guilty."

117

"The paint color."

"It does look nice."

She leans away from me. "You completely cheated, Rembrandt. You know what I liked and used it against me!"

And I can't believe, really can't, that she…well, that she really, maybe, *believes* me. My throat thickens. "Sorry. I know. I just didn't want to screw anything up."

She's frowning.

"Believe me, it's happened, and I'm not going into the details, but…the important part is that after I caught the coffee shop bomber, I returned to the present, and our daughter was dead."

"Oh." Her breath catches and she swallows. "What happened?"

"That's what I've been trying to figure out—"

"The serial killer. The one you've been tracking." Her mouth opens again. "The guy with the tattoo!"

"Yes." I hesitate, but only for an instant. "He kills you, too, in the future."

She opens her mouth, then presses her hands to her head and gets to her feet. "No wonder you freaked out about my being at the tattoo parlor."

"Please sit down."

"Oh, God. I thought you were kidding." She rounds on me. "You are. *Serious*."

"Eve, I was here before. Two days ago. We chopped down that tree in the alleyway, and then I went and killed the man who killed you—"

"You did *what*—?"

I hold up my hand. "Just, calm down. He's still alive, because… well, he isn't the guy."

"Leo something—"

"Fitzgerald."

"You had a fight with him a few months ago." She's staring at me. "Or was that the real you?"

"I am the real—okay, never mind. No, it was me. Old me."

"Chronothizing you."

"Right. It was one of my first travels, and I thought I'd arrest him, connect him with Lauren Delany's murder, but he got away, and we didn't have the DNA we needed yet—"

"That's why you asked me to run a DNA test."

"Yes."

She's thinking, shaking her head. "Wait. So how long…do you like, pop in, and pop out, like a…are you a ghost?"

"No, I'm me. I'm just…an older version of me, in my head…"

"So, what happens to the you who is, you know, *you*?" She's still standing, and now gestures over my body with her hand.

"I think my memories assimilate. I don't know. I know my feelings do. And I think maybe I view things as if I'm outside my body, because I know that, as young me, I never knew about… well, that I was being chronothized."

She settles back onto the sofa. "This is so far beyond weird I don't know where to start."

I take a breath, because we all know that isn't the worst of it.

But overall she's handling this pretty well, don't you think?

"Eve. The reason I'm back—and this is the last time—is because your murder happens sometime during the next twenty-four hours."

I probably could have said that more delicately, but frankly, I need her cooperation if I hope to keep her alive.

"What?" She swallows, a large, loud lump in her throat.

Her hand is trembling when I take it. "The real serial killer, not Leo Fitzgerald, knows me, and I don't know why, but this has become a very personal game to him…me against him. Before ten o'clock tomorrow night, you will be taken, strangled and shoved into the trunk of a 1977 Olds Toronado."

A beat passes between us. "The same car that ran down Julia."

I should have guessed that her CSI brain would make that connection. "I'm sure they're intertwined. I was convinced it was Fitzgerald, but now…well, I was wrong."

"Because you killed him before he could kill me."

"Yes," I say softly.

She gets up then, and walks over to the fire, now flickering softly in the hearth. Stares at it a long time, the flames shadows upon her face.

Then, she turns her face set like flint. "Walk me through it. Everything I did, every piece of evidence. We're going to find him before he finds me."

Chapter 11

Rembrandt Stone didn't look like a man who'd lost his mind.

Eve sat in an overstuffed chair across from the man sleeping on the sofa, a knitted green afghan over him, his breaths in regular, deep rhythm.

No, he didn't look crazy, not unless crazy had tousled black hair, a thickening scrape of black whiskers on his chin, and wore a rumpled T-shirt and jeans.

Even his socks, half off his feet, were cute.

She'd told him she'd marry him. But that was before he'd confessed the time travel stuff. Would it have made a difference? Should it?

Besides, she almost, nearly believed him. It accounted for a lot, really.

How he knew her. How she felt like she knew him, deep in her soul, too. Had, from the first moment she'd met him. But she'd always attributed that to the fact she'd read his memoir.

She took another sip of coffee, then got up and walked back into her den where a web of facts and a sci-fi timeline decorated her walls.

Rembrandt had paced, recounted his various histories, and told her such a slew of stories, she had finally written it all down to keep it straight.

She stepped to the origin point, his first timeline, the one where his brother had been murdered and missing for seventeen years, the one where her father and brother had died in a drive-by shooting, the one where Chief John Booker was dead from cancer, and the one where he was no longer a cop, but an aspiring author.

Also, the one where they shared a beautiful daughter. This is the world he came from, the one he'd lost, the one he was trying so desperately to recreate.

She pressed her hand on the paper and closed her eyes, seeing him as he sat on a chair, his hands in his hair, hearing the brokenness of his words when he said, "She had just turned seven. We'd had a birthday party for her the night before." He'd looked up at her then, his eyes reddened, maybe from fatigue, but probably from heartbreak. "The last thing she asked me to do was find this stupid teddy bear I'd given her named Gomer. And then I came back to find that this man, a serial killer, had pulled her out of her bed and murdered her."

It was then, right then, when he swallowed, and looked away, rubbing a thumb through his eye, when she wanted to believe him.

Sure, it sounded crazy but...

Well, she might be a little crazy for this man, too.

"We're going to find this man, and stop him, Rem." As soon as he'd woken, she'd gotten up, gone over, and put her arms around him. "Tell me everything, and don't leave the smallest detail out."

He put his arms around her, then, and just held on.

"Even the parts about me."

So, he had.

He'd told her about her delivering him divorce papers on the front steps of their home, and how she'd later married Burke (and he'd ended up with Shelby). He told her about returning from the past to discover the deaths of twenty-plus women, and how he went back to save Asher and her father—and she wanted to weep at that—and then returned to realize he'd made it worse. How the killer had been given a name by then, and was known by his calling card—a twenty-dollar bill with the words, *Thank you for your service*, scribbled on the back. He recounted then how he'd rescued Burke from a burning building, and again, saved her father.

He told her why he'd fought with Leo Fitzgerald in a bar, and later tracked him down in the present, in a world where she and Rembrandt were back together, although childless. How Leo finally confessed to being the architect of the bombs that took out the coffee shops, although he hadn't known the motive behind it. He told her she'd saved his life, too, in the middle of the ocean after moving to Miami—and that's when all of it felt way too real.

Because she was considering a move to Florida.

Then, he told her how when he returned this last time, he'd thought he'd ended the nightmare.

He'd killed Fitzgerald in the now, this morning to come, in a different past, and even saved Booker from getting shot, and when he returned, he'd hoped it might all be set right.

"But it wasn't." His voice had turned tired, and he'd long ago sunk onto the floor, his back to the wall, his legs crossed at the ankles. "I'd turned into a Russian thug—"

"What?" She turned from where she was taking notes at her desk.

"I mean, I'm obviously not Russian, but…I worked for Alexander Malakov, as his right-hand guy, and it took a bit to realize I was working undercover."

"Oh no."

123

"Oh yes." He studied her, and sighed. "I didn't handle your death well."

A beat passed between them before she turned back to her notes. "About that. Tell me how I died."

"Eve—"

"Everything, Rem."

He was silent, and she looked over and he was looking at her, his jaw hard. "You were one of his victims. Strangled."

She drew in a breath.

"Not sexually assaulted."

She didn't know why—it wasn't going to happen, but still—those words loosened a fist inside her. "And. How about the twenty?"

"Yes. It was found on your body."

"Okay, then. And there's no way it could be a copycat?"

"No. No one here even knows the crimes are connected."

She stared at the array of stories, at the victims. "Where was I abducted?"

"From the street. You were on your way to work. You'd parked down the block, however, instead of the parking lot, and I still don't know why."

"Where?" She'd made him pull out a map of Minneapolis to show her. She marked it and pinned it to the wall.

"And tell me about that day."

So, he'd given her a timeline, including as much as he could remember of their conversation in the hospital.

"Why would you ask me to look up a Gio Rossi?"

He told her, and she made a note to track him down in the military database.

She'd also put the victims on another wall. Three of them she knew—Lauren Delany, a working girl from this past September, and Gretchen Anderson, a nurse. And, of course, Julia, her best friend, when she was fifteen.

Rembrandt had also listed out all the clues he'd gathered from all his, well, lifetimes.

Besides the twenty, and the strangulation, he also had info on a tattoo, connected to the Big Red One, a military unit in the first Iraq war, which she already knew about.

He'd also managed to connect a class ring to the beating of a girl named Gretta.

"Leo's mother said his team won a state championship, so I thought it might be a championship ring."

And then there was a boot print, size twelve near Lauren's body, and others, a Hollie Larue and Meggie Fox, in the future.

"But see, there are holes. Like the fact that Leo Fitzgerald is an OTR Trucker. And, you mentioned his shoe size—fourteen—doesn't fit the print."

"I sound pretty smart."

He smiled at her then, his face so drawn she knew he was fading. "You have no idea."

"And then there's Leo himself, who says he's innocent, and that he was set up by a guy named Johnny. I thought he was hearing voices, but now I'm not so sure." He closed his eyes, rubbed them with his thumb and forefinger. "Maybe I'm hearing voices."

He stared at her, then, and took her face in his hands. "The last time I saw you, alive, in my time, you told me you were pregnant. And I told you that everything was going to be okay."

She pressed her hands to his chest. "And I'm sure I believed you." Her lips pressed his, and she felt in his touch a longing that she knew she didn't deserve.

Not yet.

But someday.

"Go to bed, tough guy. It'll be okay."

Ten minutes later, he was a dead man on her sofa.

And she intended to keep her word. She scanned the stories, the board and the timelines. Seeing her choices, her future, she knew she wanted it.

With Rembrandt, a man who simply wouldn't give up on the people he loved. Maybe he was telling the truth.

She finally walked over to the map. "What were you up to, Eve?"

Why would she park on the street two blocks away from HQ instead of the ramp? Her father was always hounding her to use the basement tunnels, for safety.

Walking back into the kitchen, she dumped the grounds from her coffee maker, then refilled it and reset it.

As she listened to it drip, her phone buzzed. She picked it up.

Are you coming to church with us today?

Her mom, and maybe she would have, but there was a man sleeping on her sofa.

Okay, definitely she should. Her mother would die if anyone in the parish knew a man had spent the night at her daughter's house. Even if nothing happened.

And it wasn't the first time. Rembrandt had stayed all night in November, too, right before their first big date, right before he'd saved Burke—

Oh. That had been old Rembrandt, too. She stilled. Were any of her romantic moments with the current, young-brained Rembrandt? Or was he, um, possessed, every time he'd kissed her?

Swell.

No. Sorry, Mom. She texted back. *Working.*

You could sneak out for a service downtown, you know.

Her poor mother. Trying to keep them all on the right side of heaven. Well, it didn't hurt. She certainly believed in God, believed He watched out for them.

In fact, Rembrandt had wondered, at some point last night, if maybe God had sent him on all these journeys.

She let the question sit, not wanting to pick it up. What did she know of God's ways?

Her coffee finished brewing and she filled her cup. Set it back. Paused.

Wait.

A church. There was a *church* located on 8th street.

She went to her computer and used Yahoo to look up churches in downtown, scrolled down the list.

St. Olaf Catholic Church. She read through the list of services. Nothing matched tonight's envelope of time.

She clicked on the calendar embedded in the site and a pdf came up.

AA meetings, every night at seven p.m..

And, just her luck, one this morning, in an hour.

But...why would she attend an AA meeting?

She headed back to the den, shooting a look at Rem. He hadn't moved. Maybe she should check his breathing.

And then end up waking him? She had no doubt she'd end up tangled in his arms.

Then she'd have to go to confession as well as mass.

She laughed a little, went back to her office and stared again at the wall.

"The last thing I asked you to track down was Gio Rossi. He served in Desert Storm with the First Infantry Division, alongside Leo Fitzgerald. Leo said he died, but maybe he didn't. Maybe he's alive and well and living as a guy named Johnny."

Rem's voice, answering her questions.

First Infantry, otherwise known as the Big Red One.

What if Johnny was alive? And what if she'd found him? And what if, like so many other guys who struggled with coming back from the war, he was an alcoholic?

Maybe he's alive and well and living as a guy named Johnny.

She stilled, and her brain returned to the scene outside the tattoo shop, where Rembrandt had grabbed her, pushed her into the alleyway. Kissed her like she'd terrified him.

Now she knew why.

That's where he'd called her brilliant. Because she'd found Leo's address. And…she'd picked up a picture of his BRO squadron.

Which he copied.

A copy she still had in her desk at work.

And, from that memory a conversation rose, one she had with a now-deceased tattoo artist named Chad about his squad. *"Led by Sergeant Rossi. Big Johnny. Bravest man I know."*

Johnny Rossi. Rembrandt's instincts just might be right.

She walked out into her living room. His phone was buzzing and she picked it up, his alarm going off. She silenced it, but he was already stirring.

He blinked his eyes open, then rolled back, wincing against the sun. "Eve."

"Still here. Still alive."

He shook his head. "You have no idea how not funny that is." He grabbed her hand, and sat up, then pulled her down next to him.

"Maybe we should just hide out here."

"Can you do that?"

"I wish." He sighed. "No. I only have forty-eight hours in this body. And then, I have to go back, regardless if I solve the crime here, or not. But if I don't…well, things can get screwed up on the other side."

"What crime are you here to solve?"

"A woman named Bianca Potter. She died last night when I was chopping down the tree. Or was about to."

"So, she's dead. Were you supposed to stop it?"

"No. I…when I mess with time, there are consequences." He scrubbed his hands down his face.

"Okay, so how do you solve Potter's case?"

"It's connected to the liquor store robbery."

"Right. The one you foresaw and saved Booker's life."

He looked at her, eyes wide.

"Remember, I came over to your apartment? I accused you of being—"

"A dirty cop. I remember now. That feels like, well, a lifetime ago." He gave her a smile.

And shoot if he wasn't way too handsome this morning, despite the beat up, scruffy look.

Except. "Rem, do you remember a date where we watched all the Godfather movies over the course of a weekend?"

He frowned, then, "Wait. Yes. Maybe. New Year's Eve?" He opened his mouth. "It was at my apartment."

"Yes." She pressed her hand to his chest. "That was the first time you said you thought we belonged together."

His mouth opened. "I did?"

"Yes." She took a breath. "Was that, um, you, or old you? I mean, were you, like possessed when you—"

Rembrandt laughed, and a smile broke out, his face unencumbered, if only for a moment. "I'm not possessed, Eve."

"Okay, whatever. When you quantum leaped into your self and—"

"It was young me." He touched her face. "I fell in love with

129

you fast, Eve, even the first time around. It just took me a lot longer back then to realize I couldn't live without you. We took the long way around, but this time…this time I want to do it all together. And sure, young me might have gotten a few nudges in the right direction, but I promise…it's all me."

All him.

"Are we still in love in your time?"

He swallowed, nodded. "Wildly."

"Okay then. I think I figured out what I was doing when I was taken, uh, tonight."

"I knew you'd find it." He winked at her.

And nope she didn't need that coffee at all to wake up. Her entire body tingled.

"Where?"

"C'mon." She stood up. "We're going to an AA meeting."

His eyes widened. "Eve. I promise, I'm not—"

"Stop." She took him by the shoulders. "I've found Johnny Rossi, from the Big Red One."

"What!" He blinked. "You found Johnny? Leo's Johnny?"

"The very one."

He smiled at her. "Eve, you're brilliant."

His words swam through her just like the first time, settled deep. "Yeah, I know."

"How did you figure it out?"

"I'll tell you on the way. Get your coat. And give me the keys. It's my turn to drive the Jeep."

CHAPTER 12

First, let's say that I was right about Eve—always have been, especially when she leads me down the path of her own hunches, one that lands us outside this building in the heart of Minneapolis.

I'm standing outside a very non-Catholic looking Catholic church that has a style that will someday be contemporary again, in my time. But the mid-century modern feel of the building seems caught between two worlds—the contemporary nudge from those who built it in the 1950s, and out of date for the parishioners of today. Sort of how faith feels to my generation, I think.

The last time I was in church, in real life, was a few months ago, for Easter. Mom and Dad invited Eve and me and Ashley out to the farm, and we went to our family's Lutheran church.

I'm not unfamiliar with the routine, having grown up in that church, at least until my brother went missing and my parents' faith began to fray around the edges.

I glance at Eve, then back to the church. I'm not surprised she brought me here. I knew she'd be able to find us the right place.

"Have you ever been to an AA meeting before?" I ask Eve, taking her hand as we walk in, as if it's the most natural thing in the world.

Frankly, and let's be honest, I don't know if any of this is going to work. I might return and Eve will have run off with the lead singer of Styx, so I'm holding onto her as long as I can.

We pass through a beautiful array of stained glass blocks into the entry, past an alcove filled with tiers of red votive candles, some of them lit under a statue of the Virgin Mary. A crucifix hangs next to a plaque on the wall.

If we confess our sins, he is faithful and just, and will forgive our sins and cleanse us from all unrighteousness.

The verse pings inside me, then falls away as I follow a sign down a hallway to a meeting room.

I peek into the sanctuary on the way, a little impressed by the floor to ceiling pipe organ behind the altar.

The meeting room is large, with a fireplace and red stackable chairs arranged in a circle. Round tables are pushed away, but one of them holds coffee.

I make a beeline to the coffee, trying to act like I belong here.

But in truth, the moment I walked in, the heebees crackled through me.

As if I'm *supposed* to be here. And at the same time, maybe not. I don't know why my innards are waging war. I'm here to find someone who might have served with Leo Fitzgerald. And more importantly, Johnny Rossi.

I fill my foam cup with black coffee, still trying to shake myself awake.

Maybe I did have a slight concussion because I slept like the dead on Eve's sofa. I wasn't even sure what world I'd woken up into when I opened my eyes.

Except, Eve was there, and any world she's part of is one I'll happily live in.

Eve has found us two seats in the circle, and pats the chair next to her as I walk over, carrying my coffee.

A large man in an army jacket and a pair of canvas jeans sits down beside me. Sticks out his hand. "Almanzo Perkins. You a first timer?"

"Yeah." I shake his leathery hand—I put him in his mid-fifties, so not old, but with seasoning in the lines of his face, in his eyes, a little salt in his thick black hair. He reminds me a little of Samuel L. Jackson, the actor, including a pair of round spectacles.

"Good to have you. Mark is our chairperson for the day. You don't have to talk, but Mark will call on you, just so he can get everyone to talk. And maybe keep Lizzy over there from dominating." He glances at a larger woman with an oversized white sweatshirt and leggings who is talking to the thin, older man next to her. "She gets a little too descriptive when we're in a Step meeting."

A Step meeting? My confusion must show because Almanzo hands me a book he's holding. It's blue, the title, *Twelve Steps and Twelve Traditions*, embossed in gold on the front.

"We're on Step Seven," he says in a whisper as a man sets his chair in the center of the circle.

He's clean cut, wears glasses, and is bald. Shaved instead of natural, although my guess is he was headed that direction given the shaving pattern. He's wearing a sweater over a pair of black jeans. Has to be Mark. Brown eyes scan the group, give me and Eve a nod, then continue on.

He starts by reading a card, which sounds like a disclaimer about the purpose of the group. Then he puts the card down and the group stands and breaks into a memorized prayer.

Funny, I know it too, at least the first part, and I find myself standing, drawn into the recitation. "God, grant me the serenity to accept the things I cannot change, courage to change the things I can, and wisdom to know the difference."

I don't know why, but the words land with a thump in my soul, as if a boot settling down into the soil.

This is my problem. I cannot accept the things I cannot change.

Eve has slipped her hand again into mine. I swear that woman can read my mind.

I don't know the rest of the prayer, however, and listen to Almanzo's deep baritone recite the rest.

"Living one day at a time, enjoying one moment at a time; accepting hardship as the pathway to peace; taking, as He did, this sinful world as it is, not as I would have it; trusting that He will make all things right if I surrender to His will; so that I may be reasonably happy in this life and supremely happy with Him forever and ever in the next."

I'm just a little undone as they chorus Amen, all fifteen of them, and sit down.

Eve tugs me down, too.

Living one day at a time.

Taking the world as it is, not as I would have it.

Trusting that He will make all things right…if I surrender…

It sounds like a time traveler's prayer, doesn't it?

My pulse is deafening, but I am glued to my chair when Mark motions to another attendee. A blonde woman in her mid-thirties, wearing a black sweater and dress pants—maybe she just came from mass—pulls out a different blue book and reads from a chapter.

It sounds like a testimony about the effectiveness of AA, if a person is brutally honest with themself, if they admit to their powerlessness to change, and if they turn their will over to a higher power.

Huh. I had no idea AA was so religious, although the end of

the reading does leave room for God, as we understand him.

I understand him to be a little bit aloof, and maybe not paying attention. Or at least that was my view growing up with a brother who'd been abducted and declared dead.

Recently, I've started to believe God might be a little more involved, and frankly, that not only scares my hair straight, but I somehow feel we're in a sort of time-travel wrestling match.

He definitely won every round so far.

I let go of Eve's hand and sit back, my arms folded. We should have arrived earlier, talked to Mark, hopefully nabbed the name of an attendee who might have served, and sneaked out.

But now we're trapped while another person reads through a list of promises from the book.

Things like, finding newfound freedom and peace. About not regretting the past, comprehending the word, serenity, and my personal favorite, suddenly realizing that God is doing something for us that we could not do for ourselves.

Then Mark asks if there are any newcomers. Eve nudges me, but my arms are locked, thank you.

His gaze lands on Eve and me, and she succumbs with a short introduction. "I'm Eve Mulligan and this is my fiancé, Rembrandt."

Fiancé. A warmth sweeps through me. I cock my head at her. She winks.

"Welcome," Mark says, "We're glad to have you here."

We're the only newcomers, apparently.

Mark then opens a copy of the book Almanzo gave me. "We're on Step Seven, about humility."

Wonderful. This will be fun.

Mark reads the chapter, and I'm thinking about the cookie I didn't grab next to the coffee, and how much of my cup is empty, but a glance at Eve tells me her entire focus is on Mark.

Fine.

"The handicap that cripples us is our lack of humility," Mark says, looking up from the text. "Our personal wants are not the point of our lives. It's about the character we build along the way. The people we become. But whenever we looked at the cost of becoming better people, we chose comfort instead. We simply didn't want to go through the hard things."

He's not looking at the book now, but at each of us. And there's murmur of agreement from the disciples.

I don't know. As a cop I spent years putting my own comfort aside, for justice, for truth.

He looks down at the book again and reads a passage about how we try and control our lives through intelligence and individual strength, and I'm confused because...isn't that what life is about?

I want to raise my hand and ask some questions, but he continues with something that, okay, makes me lean forward.

"We've all learned that we can't break free of our defeats and humiliations. We can't do it on our own. Only through humility can we find true freedom. True serenity."

He closes the book. "Listen, I get it. Reaching for the bottle is all about wanting to run from pain. From problems. From the fact we just can't get it right." He pauses. "Have you ever considered that maybe, you're just running from yourself?"

He's scanning the room again, and I lean back, and study the food table.

"If we're honest, the chief reason we reach for the bottle, or anything else, is fear. Fear we will lose something we love, or fail to get something we want. But in acting out our fear, we've only achieved more pain, more destruction."

Crap. Now I'm listening. How can I not? I want to look

around and see if Booker is here, or maybe Art, standing in the wings. Especially when Mark puts the book on the floor and concludes with, "Don't be afraid of the journey. It's just as important as the destination."

My thoughts are caught back on the serenity prayer. *Living one day at a time. Taking the world as it is, not as I would have it. Trusting that He will make all things right...if I surrender...*

"What if, in that moment of fear, we reached out to our Higher Power instead? The seventh Step is about stepping into a state of honest humility, understanding that there is grace to be found in surrender."

I can see Eve staring at me out of the corner of my eye. I turn and fix my eyes on her gaze. And suddenly I can't breathe.

"Would anyone like to share today?"

That does it. I'm out of here.

I don't even grab Eve's hand, I just lurch out of my chair, head to the door, push through, stride out into the hallway, lean over and grab my knees.

Of course, she's through a moment later, but I think I've successfully pushed my heart back into my chest. Still, what just happened in there?

"Rem? Are you okay?" She touches my arm.

"Yes." No. I stand up. "Let's just...can we leave?"

She's looking at me with more than a little concern. I guess she's right—I did bolt out of the meeting like I'd see a ghost.

No. Just a reflection of myself.

Honest humility, huh. I look at her, this woman I love more than my soul, and I'm finding it harder and harder to lie to her.

"I'm an addict," I say.

She frowns. "What?"

"Not like—" I gesture to the door. "I mean, I don't drink—I

mean, I did, I think, but, I'm—that guy. The guy living in fear, trying to solve everything on my own. Trying to get it right, over and over and over and…" My throat is tight, and now I can't breathe again. "What if I don't get it right, Eve? I'm caught in an endless cycle of trying to rewrite my life, our lives, and … what if I *never* get an ending I can live with? Except even then, it's not the right ending—it'll never be the right ending." I think I'm crying now because my voice breaks. "I've lost it all—you, Ashley, our home, my life—I had a happy ending and I *didn't see it.*"

I breathe out again and turn, brace my hands on the wall, shake my head. "I was afraid." I look at her. "Afraid I'd lose it all. It's why I left the force. I was afraid I'd get killed and Ashely would never have a father, so I walked away from…myself. The person I was supposed to be…" I cut my voice low. "Booker was so right."

And I know she has no idea what I'm talking about, really, but she's saying nothing, just listening, her hand on my back.

"I should have never left the force. I liked what I did. I believed in the mission—to make the world a better place, by finding justice."

"It is biblical," she says quietly.

I glance at her.

"What does the Lord require of you but to do justice, and to love kindness, and to walk humbly with your God?"

I stare at her.

"C'mon. My mother never let us skip mass."

But I can't dislodge her words. Walk *humbly.*

Yeah, that's never been my theme song.

I stand up. "What if God gave me the watch?"

She frowns.

"What if he's the one that's behind this, all of it?"

"I don't…" She shakes her head.

But another thought has hit me. "The Jackson killer read my memoir."

"What?"

I cut my voice low because, well, "Your body is found in Minnehaha Park, the place where—"

"Your first investigation took place," she says. "Wow. You're right—this *is* personal."

"Yes." I look at her, my mind spinning, searching for motivation. "What if he thinks I'm arrogant, like your father—"

"My father?"

"He hated my book."

"Oh, I don't think he hated—"

"*Hated*, Eve. Remember, I know him. You don't know about the great Thanksgiving Dinner fight of '02, when he told me I was an arrogant liar who could have gotten people killed."

She looks appropriately horrified. "My dad said that?"

"Says. Future." And I don't add that he was probably angry about the fact we'd moved in together, without the benefit of marriage. Still, "But that's the point. He thought I was arrogant. And if he thought it, maybe the Jackson killer does too. Maybe that's what this whole game is about... humility." I look back toward the group, through the glass of the door, and they've disbanded, a few standing near the cookies. Almanzo is talking with the blonde.

"C'mon." I grab her hand and press the door open. The conversation dies, ever so briefly as we head over to Mark, talking with Lizzy.

He turns. Shakes my hand.

"Sorry," I offer.

"That happens sometimes." He smiles. "You okay?"

"Yes." Maybe. "But we do need your help."

"Anything."

"We're looking for a man named Johnny Rossi. He's former military, with the First Infantry, served in Operation Desert Storm, and I think he might attend your meetings."

He swallows, and his gaze goes over to Almanzo who is looking at us, too.

Mark shakes his head. "I don't think—"

"I know Johnny," Almanzo says, coming over. "I'm his sponsor."

I can't believe it. It's like we walked right into the arms of fate.

Humility. Again the thought strikes me that, what if I'm *not* actually at the helm of all this?

"We need to talk to him," Eve says. "It concerns...well, a missing woman."

I know she's talking about herself, and for some reason, I find that funny. I glance at her, but she's not smiling.

Right.

"I'll call him. He's usually working at this hour, but, maybe." He steps away and I look at Eve.

Now, she smiles.

"If you ever need to talk about...well, anything that might help you on your journey to recovery, feel free to give me a call." Mark hands me a card.

"Thanks." I pocket the card and Almanzo walks over.

"He'll talk to you, although he doesn't know anything about a missing woman."

Not yet, he doesn't. My blood is hot in my veins, however, and I take a breath. Just calm down, Rembrandt.

Let's remember that right now, in the past timeline, I was pressing a pillow to Leo Fitzgerald's throat as he bled out in his living room, thinking I'd just caught—and killed—a serial killer.

And now, Eve and I have tracked down, well, maybe the real

killer.

This could all be over. Today. Now.

Before Eve is taken.

Before Ashley is murdered.

I know I'm getting ahead of myself, but I can't help it.

Please, God.

Hey, stop judging me. I'm in a church. It's the right place for a prayer.

"He's a security guard at the Luxeford Hotel."

Right. In my time, it's the Doubletree, but I remember the remodel. It's just a few blocks away on LaSalle.

Eve seems to know where it is, too. "Thanks," she says to Almanzo.

She's quiet as we walk out to the Jeep.

"Are you okay?"

She still has my keys and climbs in the driver's side.

"I'm about to meet the guy who might kill me," she says when I get in.

"Eve." I touch her arm. "You know I won't let that happen, right?" But my heart is thundering, too.

Johnny is *alive*, just like Leo said. And I don't know why he's been playing a game with me for twenty-three years, but I'm about to find out.

He's going down for the murders of Lauren Delany, Gretchen Anderson and Eve's friend, Julia Pike.

We drive over to the hotel in silence. Eve pulls up to the plain brown bricked building. I see a sign in the doorway—future home of the Doubletree—and it's a little weird to see that I'm right.

The lobby is in need of repair, the gold drapes shabby, the wood of the reception area chipped, the white tile dull.

Eve asks the receptionist with big hair and a dark green vest about Johnny Rossi, and she points to a man standing by the elevators.

Sure. I saw him when I walked in, but my gaze slid past him.

Even now, I'm a little stymied, looking at him, trying to puzzle together what I know about Johnny.

Johnny Rossi is the half-brother of Leo Fitzgerald, who is as Norwegian as the day is long, tall, blond and white.

And Johnny, in the words of Leo's mother, is his spitting image.

Eve comes back to me, a look of expectancy on her face.

I feel sick, and take her hand, shake my head. "It's not him," I say quietly.

"What?"

"It's not him."

"You're sure?"

"Yes," I say quietly.

But we'll have to talk to him anyway because clearly, something isn't right.

The game is still afoot.

Because Johnny Rossi is young. Strong. Capable. A handsome, wide shouldered man who has skin the color of the night sky.

CHAPTER 13

Eve didn't know why she was so upset—it wasn't like she expected to catch a serial killer on her first try.

Okay, maybe she did.

Admittedly, the entire idea that in a few hours she would be kidnapped and killed had her more rattled than she wanted to admit.

She was simply overreacting. After all, now that she knew about it, it wasn't going to happen, right?

They were sitting in the lobby as they talked with Johnny-who-wasn't-Johnny, a man named Johnny Ricardo who had agreed to answer their questions. She saw the former soldier in him when he called her ma'am, his politeness when Rembrandt asked him for help.

"Yes, I served in the First Infantry," he said now. He wore a suit and tie, a radio on his belt, and although she saw no weapon, he seemed capable. Good looking, dark skin, solemn eyes. "That's probably why Manny thought it was me. But I don't know anything about a missing girl."

Of course not. Because she hadn't gone missing yet.

Stop. She wasn't going to let the Jackson killer find her, strangle her and put her in a trunk of a car.

Wasn't going to let the same man who killed her best friend also end her life.

Calm down, Eve.

Rembrandt's behavior at the AA meeting hadn't helped. He'd been upset about something. Although, Mark's words about fear kept pulsing through her, too. *In acting out our fear, we've only achieved more pain, more destruction.*

She didn't want to act out in fear. Didn't want Rembrandt's words about finding her body in Minnehaha Park turn her cold, cause her to make mistakes.

So, she kept her voice even when she asked, "Do you have a tattoo?"

He looked at her. "No, ma'am."

Shoot. Definitely not their guy.

"Did you know a guy in the Big Red One named Leo Fitzgerald?" Rembrandt asked.

"Sure. Good guy. Quiet. He's from Minnesota too—was in Basic with me. And, we served in the same platoon."

"What do you remember about him?" Rembrandt asked. He sat on the edge of the sofa, leaning forward, pressed into Johnny's words.

She should feel safe—Rembrandt was on the job.

Outside, the wind had started to whip up, snow skirting off the tops of piled banks. Her mind wandered back to the murder he'd talked about last night—the woman found in an alleyway.

Any murder was horrible, but to be left in an alley, or in the trunk of a car—

"Fitz put his head down, did the work," Johnny said.

"Was he a ladies' man? Did he visit the working girls off base?"

Johnny shook his head. "Not that I can remember."

"What about a guy named Big John?" Eve asked, and Rem looked at her. She shot him a trust-me look. "I talked to a guy named Chad, down at Midtown Ink, and he served in the BRO."

"Yeah," Johnny said. "Sure. I see him now and again at a bar the guys like to hang out at. It's outside the city, run by an old Vietnam vet."

"In Montrose?" she asked.

Johnny nodded. "Yeah, that's the one."

She looked at Rem who gave her a slight nod. "Tell us about Big John."

"Now *he* liked the ladies. Would go in every weekend, if he could and, well, you know." He rubbed his hands together. "Not my thing."

She knew she liked him.

"He was a joker, Big John was. He'd play tricks on the guys, sometimes get them blamed for something they didn't do—like once he superglued the sergeant's boots to the floor. Thought it was funny that we all had to do pushups until the sergeant got the boots free."

"Sounds like a real gem."

"Yeah. He'd leave twenty-dollar tips for the girls in town with the words, *thank you for your service* written on it. Thought it was real funny because it's something everybody says to us, you know? Thank you for your service. Wink wink. Crude, if you ask me."

Rembrandt was staring at him. "It wasn't Leo who left the twenties?"

"He was still broken up about some girl back home. No, it was Big John that did the bills trick. And then some of the other guys did it—it sort of took off. But then our CO caught wind of it, and he thought it was crude, too and shut it down. But it didn't

145

matter because about then their squad was out on patrol and…"

He made a face.

Rembrandt stilled. "Big John's squad."

"Yep. Roadside IED. Ambush. The first Humvee blew up, then the next one was shot at. Half the squad died. The rest ended up stateside, in Walter Reed."

"Leo?"

"I think so. Maybe just PTSD, but I think he might have had a head injury."

"And Big John?"

Johnny ran his hand across his mouth. "I don't know. Maybe that's why Leo was so broken up. They were cousins. Big John watched his back. I can't remember what happened to him."

"Leo and Big John were close."

"Yeah. Like brothers, even in boot camp."

"Thanks, Johnny," Rembrandt said, standing up and holding out his hand.

"What does this have to do with a missing girl?"

"Everything." Rembrandt looked at Eve. "You might have just saved her life."

Eve thanked him too, and then followed Rembrandt out to the Jeep. She sat in the driver's seat and turned on the heat.

He was thinking—she could nearly see the gears moving in his brain. "What?"

"I need to talk to Leo."

She drew in a breath. "The last time you two talked, you, um…"

"Killed him. Yeah." He turned to her, and she saw in his gaze the reason she'd always been intrigued, even mesmerized by Rembrandt Stone. That intensity. That passion. That surety of purpose. She saw it during their first case, and in every case after that. And sure, he might be his older self, but his younger self had it too, just in its rawer form.

She could see why her father might call it arrogance.

She called it driven.

His story from the church flashed back to her. *I walked away from…myself. The person I was supposed to be…*

Yeah, well, not on her watch.

He might be about changing the past. But she was going to change the future.

"I won't let you kill Leo," she said quietly.

He frowned.

"Because I'm going with you."

His expression changed, hardened and she didn't have to be a time traveler to know what would emerge from his mouth next. "No. Absolutely not."

"Rem. He's not the Jackson killer."

"Yes, but that doesn't mean he's not dangerous."

She put her hand on his arm. "You said you wouldn't let anything happen to me."

He drew in a breath. Looked away.

"Have a little faith, Rem."

He looked at her, his jaw tight. And then, as he stared at her, his jaw slacked. "They hang out at the Montrose bar."

"Yes."

"What if Big John was there, the day I beat up Leo? Remember what Johnny said about him being protective? Maybe that's why he's been hunting me."

"If he's still alive."

"Let's go talk to Leo." And then he smiled, and she felt it to her bones. "You're right. This chat is going to go much differently."

She put the Jeep into reverse. "Why?"

"Because I'm going to give Leo what he wants…" He took a breath. "I'm going to believe him."

He was silent, staring out the passenger window of the Jeep as she drove out of the city, toward Montrose. "I've been wrong for six weeks, and twenty-three years."

She glanced at him. "Rem. The clues line up. Leo has the tattoo. His DNA matches the DNA found on Lauren Delany's body, and Gretchen Anderson's body. You said his stepfather drove a Toronado—possibly the same kind of car that ran down Julia. He *dated* Julia. And Lauren. And Gretchen. I see a pattern here."

"All three women broke up with him," Rembrandt said. He turned to her. "And remember what Johnny said? Big John was protective of Leo."

"So, what are you saying? That Big John killed those girls because they hurt Leo?"

He drew in a breath. "He said something…last time. Before we fought. He said that Johnny killed them all."

She said nothing.

He shook his head. "I should have believed him."

"You know better than I do that people will say *anything* to get out admitting guilt."

He nodded.

She debated, then, "How did it happen? You know, last time."

He looked at her. "How did I kill him, you mean?"

"Was it an accident?" And she didn't know why she was holding her breath. Why she suddenly wanted a yes.

"Yes, but…" he said quietly. "If it hadn't been an accident, I don't what would have happened."

Oh.

He looked away from her. "He told me that Johnny would never stop. That *he* couldn't stop him." He paused. "And then I made him angry and he said something I couldn't …" He drew in a breath. "I couldn't let him get away."

"Rem?"

He shook his head.

She drove, could almost hear the churning inside him.

"He told me I deserved for you to die. That he hoped Johnny would kill you."

Her body stilled.

"Even with that, I knew it was wrong, Eve. But I kept thinking that if I did this wrong thing, I could fix so many evils. Make so many things right. That doing something bad would pay off in good."

He was probably thinking about the words today, from Mark.

"And, for the record I didn't go in there planning on killing him." He sighed, leaned over and turned down the heat. "It just got out of control."

She didn't want to imagine him grappling for his life. Or killing someone with his bare hands. "How?"

"He had a knife."

She waited but Rembrandt said nothing else and she could imagine the rest. Or rather, didn't want to.

They passed out of Minneapolis, into the suburbs, and onto the highway that led to Montrose. She remembered driving it last time, on her way to the hospital to see Rembrandt.

Shelby had called her with the news of his fight at the bar.

It was probably the first time she realized that she'd lose her heart to this man who lived outside the lines.

She just hadn't realized how far outside.

Or, how much it really cost him. *What if I don't get it right, Eve? And I'm caught in an endless cycle of trying to rewrite my life, our lives, and I never get an ending I can live with?*

149

She touched his arm. "We'll find him, Rem. The Jackson killer. I promise."

He covered her hands with his. "Me too."

They rode in silence until he directed her toward Leo's neighborhood. The sun was high, almost noon, and a semi-truck cab was parked in front of a ranch house. The owner still hadn't removed their Christmas lights—they sagged from the gutters, and a clump of plastic that used to be a snowman cluttered the front porch. Someone had plowed, however, because tall banks lined the driveway.

The house of busy, tired people.

"It doesn't look like his mother is home. She has a little Ford Fiesta, but it's not in the drive," Rembrandt's voice held a hitch.

"I'm going in there with you."

He turned to her, touched her arms, his grip tight. "If he gets violent, you leave. Call 911. But whatever you do, don't get involved." His gaze turned fierce, made even more so by the bruises around his eye. "I know how to take care of myself. But I'm no good if you get hurt, okay? Even if he isn't the Jackson killer, he did—*does*—try to kill me. He has it in him."

She nodded, her throat tight.

The got out and walked up the drive. Stood at the door.

He took her hand. Squeezed it.

Then he knocked.

CHAPTER 14

We've been here before, haven't we? You remember—I rang the doorbell like a perfectly calm person, and I had good intentions—I did. But things went way south.

Ever have that dream that you're reliving your past conversations? Yeah, that one where everything moves in slow motion, and you know everything before it happens?

This is that dream, only worse because now Eve is here to witness it.

But this time we will not fight.

No one is going to die.

Eve has my hand in a death grip, however, and I don't know if that's for me, or for her.

I'm running through the panicked conversation from the night, a few lifetimes ago, when I confronted Leo in my broken living room, in the present. He'd just escaped from jail. Eve was missing. And his words, *Johnny killed her,* now echo again in my head.

The door opens. Leo is standing there. He looks tired, and I remember he's just arrived home from a long haul. His short blond hair is shaggy, and he's wearing jeans and a sweatshirt. I'd forgotten that he's taller than me, too. "You," he says.

This can go two ways, right?

I go in, loaded with accusations. Or I play this differently. *We can't do it on our own. Only through humility can we find true freedom.*

"Can we talk? I need your help."

He frowns. Hangs on the door. "Why? You gonna jump me again?"

And we both know he's referring to the fight at The Joint, a couple months ago, and not the one that played out in a different timeline. Still, his words sort of hit me.

He *can't* know, right?

"I think I got the wrong guy." I say that for the fight that hasn't yet—and won't—happen. Even so, the words burn a little on their way out.

He stares at me, and his mouth tightens.

"I know you didn't kill Lauren Delany and Gretchen Anderson."

His mouth gapes a little and then he frowns, looks past me, then at Eve. She has put on her CSI badge, with the Minneapolis Police identification on it, so he knows who he's talking to.

"Yep. We know it wasn't you," she says, playing along. "But we just need to clear up a few things."

He hesitates, then nods and opens the door.

And, we're in.

The aroma of coffee fills the house, and I remember having a cup of Joe with his mother, a few days ago in a past life. She told me how Lenny, as she calls him, came back from the war altered, and I'm guessing it was seeing his squad murdered that gave him that diagnosis.

Leo pulls a pack of Camels from the pocket of a brown canvas jacket hanging from one of the chairs in the kitchen, then sits down and lights his cigarette. Blows out a ring of smoke. "What things?"

Eve is behind me, where I prefer her at the moment, but she speaks first. "See, we have this problem. A few years ago, a girl was murdered—Julia Pike. I think you knew her."

His looks away, nods.

Against my better judgment, she sits down. "Leo, I was Julia's best friend. She told me about this guy she had a thing for. Told me he was sweet and kind to her, and that she was falling for him."

I look at her. This was not on my agenda of topics, but she's softened her tone, and I'm oddly reminded of the time she tried to get our daughter Ashley to confess to breaking one of the Christmas ornaments off the tree.

Even I can't withstand Eve when she talks like this.

"She loved you, Leo. And I think you loved her, too."

He takes another drag on his cigarette. His hand is shaking.

"So, I know you couldn't have killed her; run her down, broken her, and left her in a ditch to die."

He swallows.

"It was a Toronado that ran her over."

He takes a breath, and silence finally causes him to nod.

"The one owned by your stepfather."

He says nothing.

"But you weren't driving."

He meets her eyes, then. Shakes his head. Turns away. There's a deep sadness on his face I didn't expect.

I take a step back, fold my arms, lean against the wall. I'm close enough to stop him if decides to take a leap at Eve. "It was Johnny, wasn't it?" I say quietly.

I know I'm cheating. He doesn't remember a fight where he confesses this. Where he told me that Johnny killed them all.

Unfortunately, even then, I thought Johnny lived in his head. He looks at me.

"I know you loved her," I say. "Just like I know you loved Gretchen, and maybe even Lauren. So, why does Johnny take them away from you?"

His eyes are reddening, his breathing fast and he takes another long pull on his cigarette. "He says that it's just him and me. That we're brothers, and that brothers…they stick together."

"But he lets you take the blame for their murders," Eve says, and it's like she and I have rehearsed this. "Just like he did back in the military. Makes everybody else do the pushups for the things he did."

Leo goes silent, but again, as if we're in each other's head, neither of us speak.

Finally, "He was just … having fun."

Eve draws in a breath. I put a hand on her shoulder.

"He wasn't just having fun when he murdered Julia," I say, for Eve.

"She was going to break up with me. Her father said we couldn't see each other."

Eve is stiffening under my hand. *Stay calm, honey.*

"And Johnny just wanted to protect you. Keep you from getting hurt. He did that too, didn't he, Leo? He protected you in basic. And even when that IED went off, didn't he? What did he do—did he pull you out of the rubble before you were shot and killed? Did he save your life?"

A look flashes over Leo's face. Nailed it. Leo looks up at me.

"Why did he want everyone to think he was dead if he was a hero?"

154

He shakes his head, but his face is crumpling now, and he puts his head in his hands. After a moment, his voice emerges raw and stripped. "They were screaming. A couple were caught in the burning Humvee, but the other guys—they'd gotten out. They were on fire, and we couldn't get to them, and he said…" He pauses. "He said that…" His shoulders start to shake. "He said they were suffering, and we were pinned down and we couldn't just let them burn to death so…"

He looks up. "I didn't want to, but he said we had to, so…"

I still. "Leo, what did you do?"

"I didn't do it. But he…" he nods. "He *shot* them."

Eve is staring at him, and she's gone white. "He shot his own men."

Lenny came home…altered. Disturbed.

Yeah, you think?

"I wasn't…" He looks up. "I can't remember much after that. Just that, he switched the ID tags."

"He did what?" I say softly.

"Johnny switched the ID tags with another guy in our unit. He said he didn't want to be in the army anymore. He was shot in the shoulder, so we knew he would be choppered out…so he switched them. After he got on the med chopper I didn't see him again for a long time."

"You thought he was dead."

"I wanted him to be!" He looks up at me, his eyes a little wild and I give into the instinct to move in front of Eve. His breath is hitching. "He showed up and told me that if I ever told anyone…" He looks away. "He's my brother."

Silence.

"Leo," Eve says. "How did Johnny get the Toronado from your stepfather?"

155

Leo frowns at her. "Nick gave it to him."

"Why?" I ask.

"Because he was his uncle. His mother's brother. He was like his dad, too. Because, you know, we didn't have a dad."

Nick Latsky was Johnny's uncle.

And then I can't breathe. I want to put my hands in my face. Then I want to shake my head in disbelief of my own stupidity.

"Leo," I say quietly. "Does Johnny still come by to see you, sometimes?"

He wears the truth in his eyes, and my gut is a knot, because I *know* Johnny. And you do too. We've met, you know, more than once.

But just to be sure, I ask him the same thing I did last time. "Why did you fight me, in the bar, Leo?"

He blinks at this, then takes a breath and drops his smoke into the cup. It sizzles. "I thought you were there for someone else."

Same answer as before, but now I get it.

"You thought I was there for Johnny, didn't you?"

He nods. "He said you were a cop and wanted to arrest him."

"For the coffee shop bombings."

His mouth opens.

"I know you built the bombs, Leo."

He looks at Eve and she gives him a grim nod.

He is about to get up, but I raise both my hands, palms up. "Take a breath there. We're not arresting you. Yet. We're just talking."

He sinks back down. "I didn't know—"

"I know. Johnny asked you to build the bombs. He asked you to plant them."

"I didn't plant them. I just...I just built them. He gave them to someone—I don't know who."

Whom. But I don't correct his grammar. Instead, I ask the question we all dread. "Leo. Does Johnny go by the name of Gene?"

He stills, and I know I'm about to be ill.

Leo gives a slight nod.

Eve stares at me, horror in her eyes, but she knows I'm right.

"Gene Latsky?"

Leo nods again.

Like I said, I'm such an idiot. Running my hand across my mouth, I turn away, walk over to the window. Stand by the coffee table I broke in the previous timeline. I might just be standing in the exact same spot where I pressed a kitchen knife into Leo's throat.

Where I killed the wrong man.

I'm shaking.

"Leo," Eve says softly. "If you are willing to tell us what you know about Gene, and his involvement in the murders of Julia, Lauren and Gretchen, I think we can talk to the DA about your involvement in the bombings. This doesn't have to destroy your life."

She's so good with people.

I close my eyes.

Gene Latsky. My physical therapist. Who fixed me up after I was stabbed by Ramses Vega, after I thwarted the CityPerk bombing.

Gene Latsky, who looks like Leo—his spitting image—who was at the CityPerk bombing and watched me stop it.

Gene Latsky who would have been killed by Leo's faulty bomb construction, if I hadn't stopped the bomb from exploding.

And Gene Latsky, who possesses a signed copy of my memoir.

When I close my eyes, I can still hear our conversation.

Think you'll find him?

We were in his office. I'd seen something in his eyes, even

then. A dare. A challenge.

A game.

I didn't know why, but I met his gaze. *"Yes. Yes I will. He'll make a mistake, and when he does, I will be there."*

I still remember the smile. Something smug. Almost a smirk. Then he said, *"I'm sure you will."*

I open my eyes. My mind is on fire. And I want to hurt someone.

But not Leo.

And I won't go after Gene. Not yet. Not until I have him cold.

Gene, you're going down for the murders of thirty-eight women, my wife and my daughter.

It's over.

Now I just have to make it stick.

CHAPTER 15

"Eve? Are you all right?"

She was standing at the window of the SCI lab, staring out into the whitening afternoon. The wind had kicked up and piled drifts along the buildings three stories below.

She turned at the voice. Rembrandt held a cup of coffee from the machine out for her, doctored, probably with creamer and sweetener, just how she liked it.

Because he knew her. Because he was her husband, in a future life.

Yeah, she was most definitely losing her mind.

She took the cup of coffee, her stomach roaring to life.

"I should have snagged you a Snickers bar, too," he said, blowing on his own cup of coffee.

Something about him had changed in the two hours since they'd taken Leo Fitzgerald into custody in connection to the bombings this summer. He'd grown more solemn and inward focused. Rembrandt had always been focused, but now the deep quietness that radiated off him suggested he was thinking. Probably unraveling his many lifetimes to confirm the truth.

Probably still dealing with the bombshell revelation that Johnny went by the name Gene.

Gene Latsky. Dr. G, as her mother called him. If Leo was to be believed, he'd killed Julia. Lauren Delany. Gretchen Anderson, thirty-six other women, including a daughter Eve hadn't yet met and...her.

She, too, blew on her coffee. "So, what now?" Her hands had stopped shaking, finally.

"Now we build a case," he said quietly. "We get Gene in here, talk to him about his whereabouts the night Lauren and Gretchen were killed. And, if we can, the night Julia was run down."

She nodded. Across the room, Silas was at work running DNA off a sample he'd taken from the crime scene last night—the one Rem had mentioned, involving a woman named Bianca.

He also mentioned needing evidence from her car if he hoped to fix whatever had been broken in his time.

Their time.

Because she planned on living through this night.

"Do you think Gene is the one who, um," she cut her voice down, glanced at him. "Killed me?"

He made a face and lifted a shoulder. "Probably, but why? What is the motive?"

She set her coffee on the window ledge. "Okay, run through it again. What happens next?"

He too put his coffee down. "I don't know, really. Last time, after...well, after I..." He sighed. "After I left Leo's house, I went to my parents' place. I'm not sure why—I just had to talk to someone. So, I went home. And met my brother, Leonardo, for the first time."

"Leonardo? Really?"

He gave a small laugh. "Yeah. Leonardo, like the painter. My other brother was Michelangelo, so..." He lifted a shoulder. "But it's weird, right?"

"Yeah, definitely." But what wasn't weird about this whole thing? "Then what happened?"

"Shelby called me because she'd tracked down Bryce Mattson, the perp from Jin's Liquor Store robbery. He was—is—going to a monster truck rally at U.S. Bank Stadium—"

"Where?"

He made a face. "Right. The Metrodome."

It was comments like these that made her want to believe him. And she did. Mostly.

Because the alternative was just too terrible. That somehow this man that she loved—and yes, it was beyond her now—was insane.

"So, you went with her to arrest him?"

"Yes." He was oddly silent, taking a sip of his coffee and she waited for it. "He died. Terrible accident."

Oh wow.

"I dislocated my shoulder, and that's when you showed up. I think Shelby called you after I drove myself to the hospital."

Of course he did.

"What happened after I arrived?"

He frowned at her, then. "Gene Latsky came in and offered to relocate my shoulder."

She met his eyes, his gaze hard on hers. "Did something happen?"

"No. I mean, yes—I had this eerie feeling about Gene—it was the first time I thought about trying to locate Johnny. I even asked you to do a search on the name Latsky..."

"Could he have heard you?"

Her question stilled him, and his jaw tightened. He put his

coffee down and turned away from her. The way he ran his hand over his eyes had her pressing hers to his back. "Rem?"

He stared at her for a good five seconds as a look of horror slowly stole over his face. "I think I got you killed."

The thinness of his voice sent a tremor through her. "How's that?"

"Don't you get it? If he's been playing a game with me for the past eight months, and if he's figured out that I'm onto him, he'll want to play the next move. Checkmate. He takes you out, and he wins."

She turned him, grabbed his arms. "He's not going to take me out. We're smarter than he is. It's both of us, right? Partners?"

He looked at her then, a depth, a surety returning to his gaze. "Yes. Partners."

"So, let's start with a reason to get him in here," she said. "You said you saw him at the CityPerk site, before you took down Ramses Vega, right?"

"Yes."

"Then he should be on a witness list. Let's track down the file."

She headed over to her computer, the to-do list already forming in her head.

At the top was nabbing his DNA.

She set her cup down. Rembrandt stood behind her, his presence warm and radiating through her body. Truth was, she didn't mind at all the idea of him glued to her for the next thirty-six hours.

And every day after that.

She searched and pulled up the case, then opened the file. "Here's the witness report." She printed it off and noticed Silas looking at her as she walked over to the printer. His gaze fell on Rembrandt, and she remembered Rem's story from the future about how Silas had helped her *divorce* him.

Never.

Rembrandt seemed to think that Silas held a torch for her. Suddenly all his objections to Rembrandt suddenly made sense.

Still. Silas was—or had been—her best friend.

Rembrandt couldn't be right about everything. In fact, a big part of her brain was wrapping her mind around what he'd already told her. *Really,* she wanted to believe him.

But, hello, *time travel?*

She picked up the list from the printer and walked it back to her station. Rembrandt was looking at pictures from the bombing, on her computer.

"I still can't believe I missed this," Rembrandt said as she sat down on her chair.

"Missed what?"

"This." He pointed to a man standing across the street from the location, near a squad car. Blond, wearing workout gear, tennis shoes. He was talking with one of the officers.

No, he was talking with her father, Danny Mulligan. "That's Gene Latsky."

"Is he on the witness list?"

She perused it, then set it down. "Nope."

"I remember the scene, as if it were yesterday, or at least six weeks ago," he said, and gave her a smile.

The first hint that he might be starting to breathe again.

"Really, six weeks for you?"

"Since all this started, yes. Six weeks and six lifetimes."

"You must be exhausted."

He looked at her and laughed and it found her core, settled there. She liked the sound of his laughter. Sweet, deep, and freeing.

Aw, it didn't matter if he knew the future, or not. She planned on living it with him.

"Beyond tired. But it doesn't matter. Gene—or who I thought was Leo—was in the coffee shop. He *saw* me, Eve. He saw that I stopped the bombing. And that's when his obsession with me began."

"Why would he want to bomb a coffee shop?" It just didn't make sense—

"*Ramses Vega* wanted to bomb the shop, remember? In retaliation for the slave labor of the coffee plantations from his country. But he needed a bomb maker."

"How did he find…" And she looked up, at Rem. "Wait. Didn't he play soccer?"

His gaze was on her, his eyes fixed. "Yes. He played for a US team, and was on the injured list."

"Gene Latsky might have been his physical therapist."

"Mariana Vega was on the local city council at the time. It's possible she got Latsky's name from one of the local cops."

"Yes. Because he specializes in working with cops and their families," she said. "But how did he know how to build a bomb?"

"He didn't have to. Leo did, remember? He was an explosives expert."

"He was?"

"Oops." He gave her a look and lowered his voice. "Maybe that was from a different life."

"Try and focus on this life, okay?" she whispered.

He smiled again. "All day long." He leaned close, as if intending to kiss her, but she put her hand on his chest.

"So, Gene needed a bomb maker, which is why he walked back into Leo's life after disappearing for so long."

Rembrandt sighed. "He dragged Leo back into his world, and suddenly they were back in basic, and he was watching over his cousin." He took another sip of his coffee.

"Weird, don't you think? That they had such a close bond?"

"Maybe it wasn't brotherly love, but control. Gene's father cheated on his mother, over and over—something I found out last time I…" He raised a shoulder, glancing at Silas, then back to her.

"Right. So he wanted to protect Leo from getting hurt, like his mother?"

"Maybe. And then there's the twenty-dollar bills. The fact that he started using them again."

"Like you said, a game."

"With me, the rookie detective who made the best-seller list, the one who stood in his way of the final bombing. He must have been laughing the entire time we worked together after my stabbing."

"Rem. Don't—how would you have ever known?"

"How did I not see it? The ring—he's got one. And a picture of his high school football team in his office."

"What about the tattoo? The one Tobey made for the Big Red One? You said you saw it in a crime…um, in the future?"

"Yeah. A security camera snagged a shot of his upper arm. That's how I tracked down Leo." He shook his head. "I can't believe I killed him."

"You didn't." She touched his arm. "And he's going to help us. I think he's actually relieved that it's over."

Rem considered her. "He's not the only one." He reached up and touched her face, dragged his thumb down along her cheek. "Eve. I'm going to get him. Nothing is going to happen to you. Tonight, or ever."

She leaned into his hand and didn't care if Silas saw.

Rembrandt's phone buzzed, and he dug it out of his pocket. "Shelby."

He answered and Eve's entire body tightened.

Shelby, calling as predicted, about Bryce Mattson.

He sighed, looked at Eve even as he talked to Shelby. "Can you chase him down on your own?"

Eve frowned, shook her head. "I'll be fine here, Rem. I'm at the police station, for Pete's sake."

He covered the phone's mic. "I'm not letting you out of my sight."

"What do you think is going to happen?"

He raised an eyebrow as if he knew exactly what would happen.

"Go," she said. "Get this Bryce guy. Solve the case. Save the world, Batman."

His eyes widened slightly, but Shelby was obviously arguing with him on the other side.

"Please," she said quietly.

"Okay. Yes. Fine. I'll be there—but don't go in without me. And...break up your backup into two teams, so we can surround him—right. We don't need a repeat of yesterday."

Eve's gaze went to the bruises at his temple, where Bryce had beaned him with a ratchet. Made a face. She'd been so worried about him last night she'd gone over to his house to check on him. And, confront him on a few, now explained, discrepancies from the liquor store attack.

Explained because he'd known the future. Because he'd been there to stop a crime.

And had nearly gotten himself killed.

"I'll be there in ten," he said to Shelby. And hung up.

"No more," she said quietly.

He frowned as he pocketed his phone. "What?"

"No more time travel," she said. "After this one, it's over."

He stilled.

"Listen, I get it. I do. You want to solve crimes, bring justice—"

"No, actually, I mostly tried to stop the crimes from happening—"

"That's what I mean. You can't run around time trying to keep bad things from happening. You'll lose your mind. Bad things are destined to happen—that's part of life. And even if they're terrible—like losing my father. Or you, losing your brother—they happen for a reason. And I'm not just saying a cosmic reason, but something personal. In here." She pressed on his chest. "They change us. Make us stronger. Wiser. And yes, sometimes it doesn't work out that way, but isn't that up to us? How we deal with it? How we chose to face it, or not?"

He blinked at her, then drew in a breath, and nodded.

She took his hands. "Listen. I don't want to know anything else about our future. We might have a child, we might not. We might buy that craftsman, or maybe not. I want a blank slate, Rem. A future that *we* write, one moment at a time. And I don't care if it's already lived…I'm living it now, here. And I want to live it with the now Rem, even though, I also love future Rem."

His breath drew in, shuttered out. "You love now Rem?"

"I'm crazy about now Rem. I just hope he remembers how crazy he is about me."

"He will." He leaned in and touched his forehead to hers. "Are you sure?"

"Yes."

He sighed. "Okay. After this, I won't travel again."

She pressed her hand to his face, not sure why she felt this terrible ripping, suddenly, inside. But it couldn't be any other way. She couldn't live with him charging in from the future, changing things.

Putting himself in the way of known danger. He did that enough every day.

"Listen. I'm going to help Shelby, and then I'll be back and we'll bring in Gene, and interrogate him."

"What if you get hurt again? What if you run out of time? What if you don't solve the cold case, and—"

"I don't know, Eve. I'm still figuring this out."

She put her hands on his chest. "You said that if you don't solve the case, then things can get screwed up. What do you need to solve Bianca Potter's murder? That's the case, right?"

"Jimmy Daggert's DNA. Which we'll get after we pull the restraining order from Bianca Potter's glove box, from her car in the impound lot. The same car I impounded yesterday in connection with the liquor store robbery. The restraining order will give Burke probable cause to bring him in, and the rest is, well, history."

"History."

Rembrandt lowered his voice. "Future history."

"Right." He stood up. "Promise you'll stay here?"

"I will be right here when you get back. Don't get hurt."

He bent down and kissed her. Right in front of Silas. And she kissed him back.

And let him go.

She waited until he was out the door and down the hall before she glanced at Silas.

He had his eyebrow raised. "You're kissing him? At work?"

"Calm down." She looked over his shoulder at his computer screen. "Did you get a DNA match from the Potter case?"

He shook his head. "Not yet."

"Did you check her car?"

He looked at her. Lines around his eyes evidenced a long night. "No. She didn't have a car. She was attacked after getting off the bus, while walking from the stop to the bar. Then dragged into an alleyway and killed." He frowned. "Why did you think she had a car?"

She stuck her hands into her pockets. Shrugged. "Because Rembrandt impounded her car yesterday, after he discovered it was used in the liquor store robbery."

Silas rolled his chair away from the computer, looked at her. "How did he figure that out?"

She knew this part, because she'd helped him. "He traced the license plate number to a local car repair shop, where it had been stolen to use in the robbery. That's where he tracked down Bryce Mattson, where he got hurt, and then impounded the car."

Silas's mouth tightened around the edges.

"C'mon, Silas. Why do you think she took the bus?"

He nodded. "Right, okay. I'll go search the car."

"Good. Be sure to check in the glove box."

He frowned as he got up, reaching for his jacket. "Aren't you coming with me?"

She considered him, glanced outside. The impound lot was only a few blocks away. She'd be back before Rem could land his collar.

"Yes." She grabbed her jacket.

Besides, what were partners for?

CHAPTER 16

Let me just say this—if you ever get arrested, don't run.

You won't get away. Maybe at first, but I will find you. Running just increases the likelihood that someone is going to get hurt. For sure you, probably me, and maybe even some innocent bystanders.

You might even get run over by a monster truck.

Yes, you heard that right.

Run over. By a monster truck. With the bully wheels and the painted chassis to look like flames or some otherworldly dragon.

Not a pretty way to go. I know, because that's how Bryce Mattson died the first time.

The sound of engines revving blasts through the Metrodome as I enter the section across from Shelby. We've devised a quick plan, mostly from my memory of the first time around when Bryce spurted out the opposite end of the row before I could get there, ran down the stadium steps, launched himself over the railing and, despite my best efforts to save him, landed in the path of one of those big trucks.

His death on a jumbotron was forever, or at least in the

previous lifetime, seared into the minds of 20,000 people.

So, this time around, we'll play it smarter.

Thirty rows down, and in the muddy middle of an arena, two giant trucks are circling, not unlike horses at a rodeo, trying to stir up the crowd. Which is sufficiently stirred—men and women on their feet, their fists pumping, children standing on the seats, holding miniature trucks.

One of the trucks below, painted green with fire along its body and flaming from two back pipes, turns to the middle and flies over a giant berm. Mud spatters the air.

I don't understand this sport. But I'm not here for the entertainment.

I spot Bryce about fifteen rows up from the barrier to the arena, in the same seats as last time, of course. He stands to cheer, lifting his arms, wearing a full sleeve of tats and a grimy gimme cap backwards over his brown hair.

Shelby is on the other side of the row, all business in a Minneapolis PD coat over a flack jacket, her demeanor calm, but ready to pounce, depending on how he reacts.

"He's gonna run," I said to her, when we gathered in the corridor and divided up the small security force that arrived to help us. It's the best I can do to warn her of the future.

That, and position myself on the other end of the row.

He's trapped between spectators, and as Shelby advances on her side, people getting up to let her through, Bryce glances at her, then spots me. His eyes go wide.

I smile. Wave. I know, but I can't help it. My shoulder still aches, bone deep.

He pushes forward, climbing over the seats, but the fans of monster truck rallies tend toward the beefy side. He doesn't get far when a patriot hands his beer to his wife, grabs Bryce and holds him down.

The row empties out for me to get in, and we're rewriting time when I snap cuffs on him and haul him up.

Shelby has caught up. "That wasn't so hard."

Below, the two trucks have been joined by four more, and the previous history is fading into new.

Bryce no longer dies, mangled, in front of thousands. Hoo-yah.

As we haul him out, into the corridor, I check my watch. I've been gone for the better part of two hours, and my pulse is pushing me to get back to Eve.

I still can't believe we've figured it out. That Gene Latsky has been watching, even baiting me, since the coffee shop bombings. I'm sure, in my soul, that he died in our original timeline, although my history is so jumbled, I can't remember now the original victims. Seems to me that a jogger was one of the eight.

Why he stopped killing after he murdered Eve in the last timeline, I don't understand.

Maybe because I stopped working homicide. He'd won.

The diabolical bastard. The sooner I get my hands on him, the sooner this is over. And with Eve's help, we have him for all three murders.

We just need his DNA.

"Take him back, and question him," I say to Shelby, who is handing him off to a uniform. "Pin him down about his accomplice."

"Are you sure he had an accomplice?"

"Dead sure," I say. "Remember his cousin? Jimmy Daggert?"

"Who?" She frowns at me, and I remember too late that the part of the investigation where we saw Jimmy's picture happened *after* Bryce died, during our conversation with his parents.

"Just tell him we know about Jimmy," I say, bypassing an explanation. "It'll rattle him into telling us the truth."

Shelby was one of the first to believe in my hunches, to take me at my word. More, she's turned out to be an excellent detective. And, since this is my last go-round in time, I stop her before she can follow Bryce out to the car. "Shelby."

She turns, and I see in her eyes an eagerness that was missing when I found her in Florida. In that time, Burke's injury had drained her.

"You're a good cop," I say. "Booker wants to know if you're ready to go out on your own…" I smile. "I told him yes. In fact, someday, you might even make chief if you keep up the good work."

She smiles, and I can see why Burke loves her. "Oh, Rembrandt. You and your big ideas. You should write fiction." She laughs.

Ha ha. I'm sure my smile is strange.

"See you back at the station," she says, and leaves.

I pull out my cell phone and dial Eve's number. It goes to voice mail, as if it's off, and that puts a craw in my gut. Maybe it died.

I notice a call from my parents, but no voice mail. I'll call them back once I know this is over.

My shoulder is aching from all the movement of wrestling with Bryce. I could use some ice, and I'm dog tired despite the catnap on Eve's sofa. I want to track down Gene, bring him in for questioning, then formally arrest him and put him behind bars.

Then I'll sleep. Because the nightmare will be over.

Eve's words about suffering dog through my mind as I trudge out to the Jeep. The sky has turned pewter, flurries sweep the air. *You can't run around time trying to keep bad things from happening. You'll lose your mind.*

Indeed. I've rewritten so many histories, they're all jumbled in my head, tangled like barbed wire.

They happen for a reason. They change us. Make us stronger. Wiser.

Maybe. I'm not the person I was when I first put on the watch. That me was running. Not on the outside—that life was settled. But on the inside, I know I'd walked away from myself, like I told Eve.

Somehow, in searching for my life, I've found what I lost. My purpose. Even, maybe, hope.

And yes, sometimes it doesn't work out that way, but isn't that up to us? How we deal with it? How we choose to face it, or not?

What if it's not our regrets that make us who we are, but the choices after the regrets?

She's right. I don't want to write my own story. There's too much responsibility to get it right.

And what does it mean to get it right, anyway? Isn't the answer not in what happens, but how it's lived?

I pull up to the police department, park in the ramp across the street, and as I walk into the main floor entrance, I'm remembering how I left my future.

Paralyzed.

Dying.

Choking on all my futile attempts to right my world.

Yes. It's over. Finally.

I take the elevator up, and get off on Eve's floor, walk into the lab.

It's empty. Silas's computer screen is spinning a Microsoft icon, and his cubicle is dark. He might have left for the day.

"Eve?" I walk in. The room is pitched in shadow, the daylight bled out of the room under a bullet sky. I walk over to her station.

Her cell phone is near her desk, dead. I pick it up, wanting to growl. But she couldn't have gone far.

She promised, right? You heard her, didn't you?

My heart is in my throat as I stalk down to the vending machines in the break room at the end of the hall. The room is dark, my fist tightening around her Nokia.

I want to shout, but I'm gulping back panic, and I don't want to go there.

Yet.

I stalk back down the hallway, and practically plow over a man coming up the back stairs near the break room.

"Whoa—Rem." Burke catches me, then takes a look at my expression because, "You okay?"

"I can't find Eve," I say, not caring what he might think.

He frowns. "Is she here?"

"No, she's not here. If she was here, then I'd be able to find her, wouldn't I?"

He holds up his hands. "Did you try her at home?"

"I was with her all night!" I say, and my voice is louder than I want. Especially since Danny Mulligan is a few steps behind Burke and comes out of the stairwell.

He looks at me. I hold up my hand. "Not now," I say.

He frowns.

"Eve is missing."

This elicits a response. "What do you mean?" Danny might be twenty-three years younger back here in the past, but he still possesses the tone of a man in charge.

"I mean I left her here two hours ago, and now she's gone."

"She's not on a leash," Danny says carefully, with a hint of warning in his tone.

I close my eyes. Hear Eve's voice about choices and reactions.

Right. I take a breath and look at Danny. "I know. I just...she said she would be here."

"She's on her way back from the impound, with Silas," Danny said. "He just called me and said they'd searched Bianca Potter's car and found a restraining order. That's why we came in."

I stare at him, my heart a fist.

Oh.

"Sheesh, Stone. Go home. You look like you got run over by a truck." Danny shakes his head.

But Burke frowns at me, and I'm remembering a sightless man who still can see me from the future. Remember telling myself that if I could, I'd tell him the truth. "I need to talk to you," I say to Burke.

He glances at Danny. "I'll meet you in the office."

Danny considers me. "I'm sure Eve will be back soon." Then he steps up to me. "I'm starting to like you. Don't make me regret it."

I want to narrow my eyes. To shout at him that Eve could have been in big trouble. That a serial killer will take her and strangle her as she fights for her life—

But as I roll those words around in my head, I realize how that sounds.

I'd get nowhere locked up in the crazy ward. I nod, my jaw tight and he walks away.

I motion to Burke to follow me to Eve's lab, praying she's materialized in my absence.

I swallow the rising tide of residual panic and walk to her workstation. Pick up the list of witnesses from the CityPerk attack that she printed out. Take a breath.

And turn to Burke.

"Remember the investigation for the coffee shop bomber last summer?"

Burke is unwinding a scarf from around his neck. I realize he's just arrived for his shift—he looks well rested and clean shaven. Which also means his head is clear.

I'm hoping that bodes well.

"Remember how I told you that I…that I came from the future, and knew what would happen?"

He stills. "Rem—"

"Just listen."

He frowns. "Okay."

"You thought I was crazy."

He cocks his head. Raises an eyebrow.

"I wasn't crazy."

I let the words settle. A beat goes by. He says nothing.

"Twenty-three years from now, you will be married to Shelby. And, if history repeats itself, you'll be blind."

He takes a breath.

"It's from an attempted hit taken out on you for killing the son of a Russian thug named—"

"Boris Malakov," he says.

I stare at him. "Yes."

He makes a noise, a grunt, deep down. "We've been tracking him. He popped up on the radar a few weeks ago, Alexander Malakov's brother, fresh from the motherland. His son is already neck deep in meth and opioid trafficking."

"Yes, well, not too long from now, you'll kill his son during a sting, and, to quote you, "If I could go back in time, I'd tell my younger self to wait for backup'."

He frowns.

"We're ambushed, you and me, and I think the way it went down is that someone got my gun and used it to shoot you."

He draws in a breath and I get it. Eve's right. No one wants to

178

know the future. Except, maybe, if it can save their life.

"And this is you, from the future, telling me this?" Burke's lips thin.

I nod. "Burke, those hunches aren't hunches. They're history. My history. Our history. I'm here because the cases we've been solving are *cold* cases."

He closes his eyes, as if in pain.

"It's this watch." I pull back my sleeve to reveal the watch. He opens his eyes.

"That's Booker's watch."

Whoops. I've just outed our boss. "Yes," I say, however.

"What are you doing with Booker's watch?"

"He gives it to me, in the future."

"Rem—"

"To solve cold cases." And, maybe, for me to see the truth.

You can't escape your calling. And if you try, it will find you.

"The watch allows me to travel, in my thoughts, to the past, and rewrite history."

He's looking me over, and I fear all he sees is a young, twenty-eight-year-old buck with probably too much arrogance, stringing up a crazy story.

And then, "What does this have to do with Eve?"

"Unless I can stop him, Gene Latsky is going to kill her."

He just blinks at me. I can see him weighing our past, the way I knew about the coffee shop bombings, the drive- by shooting at Danny's house, maybe the way I showed up to save his life, and a dozen other minute details that I know sit in his brain.

Burke is sharp. And he's also a jazz musician, which means he knows how to adapt, to see and hear fluctuations in tone and rhythm that can change the music.

Still, this is a lot to believe.

"Rem—"

"It's true," says a voice, not mine.

My mouth opens to Booker, walking into the door. I don't know how long he's been there, but he looks at Burke, then me.

Then he lifts the sleeve of his shirt and reveals his watch. The same one I'm wearing.

Burke stares at him with a sort of horror. Takes a breath. "C'mon Booker—"

"He's telling the truth, Burke. And he's running out of time," Booker says, turning to me.

I'm a little surprised by his words because I don't remember telling Booker in the now about Eve's death. Still, he's right.

Burke looks at me, then, shaking his head. "How?"

"How do I travel?"

"No. How do you know it's Gene Latsky?"

He knows him, too, so I get it. Clean cut PT, the guy who is everyone's friend. How could he kill thirty-eight women?

So I don't start there. I hand him the paper Eve printed. "This is the witness list for the CityPerk bombing. He's not on it…but…" And then I pull up the picture from Eve's computer. Of course I know her passwords, but Burke doesn't comment.

The shot of Danny talking to Gene pops up. I point to him. "I saw him in the shop. He was there."

He looks at the shot, then me. "And?"

"And we've linked Gene Latsky to both Ramses Vega and the bombmaker, a guy named Leo Fitzgerald."

He frowns, but doesn't ask how. "You're saying he helped Vega with the bombing?"

For shorthand's sake, I nod, and add, "And he knows that Eve knows."

Burke draws in a breath. "When?"

"Tonight. He takes her tonight—I told her to stay here, but she's…"

"With Silas," he says, and puts his hand on my shoulder.

It's right then that Silas walks into the lab. He's peeling off his parka, holding a plastic evidence bag with the restraining order inside.

Burke turns and we wait for Eve to follow him in.

A beat passes as Silas hangs up his coat. Turns and looks at us. "What?"

"Where is Eve?" I ask.

He frowns. Lifts a shoulder. "She said she had to do something, and she left."

I stare at him, then Burke, and he keeps his hand on my shoulder, probably so I don't leap at Silas and strangle him.

"Do you know where?"

He shakes his head, looks at Booker, then Burke.

"It's important," Burke says in his low voice.

"No. One second she was with me, the next, she'd taken off."

My throat is dry, closing in.

"Maybe she went to get a sandwich," Silas says.

Burke holds up his hand to him, turns to me. "How does it happen?"

"He takes her right off the street. But that was after the hospital…" I shake my head.

I don't know why Gene would know, now, about Eve, but time and fate don't play fair, we both know that.

I pull out my phone. And I know my common sense is spinning out, but I can't stop myself from opening up my contacts and finding Gene's number.

Yes, it's in there, from when he helped me last summer.

And stop your shouting—I just want to have a little

conversation. Player to player.

Burke frowns and steps away from me.

Gene picks up on the second ring. "Rembrandt?"

He doesn't sound like a killer who has the woman I love by the throat. Not winded, not even evil. "Good to hear from you. What's up?"

I swallow, and then, shoot, I can't stop the word from escaping my lips, my voice soft and steady. "I know it's you." I pause for a breath. "And I know you have her." I close my eyes, and shake my head at what I've just done, but it's the price I'm willing to pay. Even Silas is staring at me with a sort of horror. "Just let her go and you win. I won't come after you."

A pause from Gene, then, "Rembrandt, are you okay?"

Not even close. "This game has to stop."

And that's the moment when Eve walks through the door.

She's carrying a bag from Dayton Deli across the street, her cheeks red and chapped, and grins at me, as if she's happy to see me.

Oh no.

I hang up, even as Gene is talking.

Burke is still as I walk over to her. Then pull her to myself, hard, shaking.

"Rem?"

I close my eyes, fighting the urge to yell. Instead I hold on. Take a breath. Put her away from me. She's staring at me, her green eyes wide. "What's going on?"

"He called him," Burke says. "Gene Latsky."

"Oh, Rem," Eve says quietly. She looks past me to Burke, then back. "Oh no. You thought Gene took me."

At the very least, I've shown my hand. If he doesn't strike back, he'll run.

Burke can read my mind. "If he's not in the wind already, he will be."

"We have to go," Eve says.

I'm about to say something like, not on your life, when the phone in my hand vibrates.

I flip it open.

I expect Gene's voice, maybe, my imagination playing a thousand different scenarios. Mocking. Angry. A challenge.

Instead, "Rem? It's your father."

"Dad?" The voice shakes me out of the moment.

"Can you come out to the house?"

I still, look at Eve, then Burke. "What's going on?"

A pause, then. "Your brother is missing."

Now, we all know it's too soon for Gene to have driven out to my house and taken my brother. But fate is always two steps ahead of me, and my brain tangles on this news.

For a second, the past grabs me. Mickey is missing?

"What do you mean, missing?"

"Leo went out about two hours ago on his snowmobile and hasn't come back. And it's getting dark out. We thought you might know where he'd go."

Leonardo, the kid brother I've only met once, although it's clear the other Rem knows him quite well. He's nine years old, and my parents' farm is a labyrinth of disasters including a pond that certainly should be frozen over, but...

Great.

I look at Eve. I have maybe thirty hours left on this ticking clock, at the most.

But as soon as Silas digs up Jimmy Daggert for Bianca's murder, as soon as he's in custody, this trip ends.

And so does my hold on Gene's fate.

"My brother is missing," I say to Eve, then Burke.

And my partner, the one who still had my name on speed dial in the future, says, "I'll find Gene. Go find your brother."

I know he's right. But I still can't believe I say, "I'll be right there."

When I hang up, I nearly throw my phone.

In a moment that feels a little like a spear through my gut, I know it all comes down to choosing finding Gene, or letting another brother disappear.

We all know the answer to that.

"Rem," Booker starts, and I don't want to hear his logic. Or my own.

I round on Burke. "Promise me you'll find him."

"I promise," Burke says, his eyes flashing.

I grab Eve's hand. "You're coming with me."

She nods and follows me. "Good thing I brought sandwiches."

I've stepped back in time. And no, I'm still in my

CHAPTER 17

twenty-eight-year-old body, but as I pull into my parents' home, the one located on acreage outside Waconia, thirty miles from the cities, it is packed with cars, a couple police cruisers and searchers armed with flashlights, and I am again twelve.

Twelve years old and the last one to see my kid brother, Mickey, alive.

Twelve years old and watching my world crumble around me.

I'm shaking a little, probably the memories of that scared kid still in my veins as I close the door to my Jeep, take Eve's hand and wind our way around the litter of cars and trucks in the drive.

A man stands on the porch of our two-story farmhouse, talking into his radio. He's wearing the uniform of Waconia Search and Rescue—a thick parka, a badge sewn into his jacket, another on his wool hat. He stares at me as I walk past, but I ignore him and push inside.

My mother is in the kitchen wearing her parka, digging through the junk drawer, her wool hat askew on her head, her mittens tucked under her arms.

"Mom?"

She turns, and a beat passes between us. Last time I saw her, ironically, just a few days ago, she was the upgraded version of my broken mother. Happy, her blonde hair freshly dyed, serving pot roast, her family mostly healed.

This woman wears the past in the lines on her face, grief leaking through from where she's tucked it away.

"Mom," I say again and pull her toward me.

She's breathing hard, trying not to cry as she hangs on. Eve steps back, giving me a tight-lipped look.

"I'll find him, I promise," I say. Of course, this is what I said fifteen years ago, but this time I'm not twelve, am I?

I give a final squeeze then release her. She's holding a pair of D-sized batteries. "For the flashlight."

Taking them from her, I turn her toward Eve. "Stay here, with Eve. Don't leave this house, no matter what happens." I mean that mostly for Eve, but she looks at my mother and nods.

The flashlight is on the counter, so I grab it and load the batteries in. Look at Eve who walks over to the stove, as if to make tea, making herself at home, and I remember we spent a day here, a few months ago.

"Eve, if Gene shows up..." I know that sounds crazy—why would he? But fate is not without its tricks.

She turns to me. "I'm not without my resources."

I give her a look, but she shakes her head. "Find your brother, Rem."

Right. I turn to my mother. "Where did he go?"

She unwinds her scarf. "He went snowmobiling out across the fields. Your father took off on one of the sleds, but he lost his trail."

"Who else is looking for him?"

"A few guys from church—they're checking the ditches along the road, and a few of the trails. And the Waconia Search and

Rescue just got here. They're calling for volunteers."

She's shed her jacket and now hangs it on a chair. Meanwhile, I've suited up—pulled on my father's padded coveralls, grabbed a pair of boots by the door, my father's thick work jacket, a pair of gloves and a hat.

It's getting cold out—I see it in the swirling snow against the gray of the windows. It'll be dark soon.

"I'll find him," I say again, shoot Eve a look, then head outside.

Twilight has fallen hard in the fifteen minutes since I've arrived, but that's Minnesota in January. I pass the SAR volunteer, glancing at him. "If someone finds him, call me." My cell phone still has some life left, and I've put it on vibrate in my thick pocket.

I head out to the barn.

The snow machines are old. Easily twenty years, but you've met my father—he keeps everything that has a motor running at top performance.

We have three sleds, mostly for our deer hunting days, but also because my father had dreams of riding with his sons.

Probably still does.

I pull the cover off the 1977 Polaris RXL, an old racing model with a blue body and white stripes.

Mickey's laughter echoes in my hollowed out heart as I climb on, check the gas, and pull the cord.

It growls to life, and I sit down and gun it out of the barn, toward the field behind the house, the lone light parting the shadows. The fields are barren, just the carcasses of corn stalks bent over in submission. Far away, the closest neighbor's porch light beckons like a lighthouse.

A few other lights edge the field, other searchers.

Gunning it away from the field, I head down to a nearby

ice-covered service road, barely used in the winter.

I know where I'm going, almost on instinct. Yes, it sounds crazy, but ever since I got the call from Dad, I felt it. I know exactly where he is.

The best place to race snowmobiles is on a large forgotten lake about two miles from the house, covered in snow and dead cattails and surrounded by forest.

No one around to tell us to slow down.

I'm sure, if Leo and I are as close as my mother suggests, he knows about Parley Lake.

And the best run into Parley Lake is Sixmile Creek.

The back roads are like old shoes, and I wind through them easily, the night thickening around me, the trees skeletal in the fading light.

It's cold, the kind that finds your bones, stiffens your fingers and toes, and my ears have turned to rubber.

Hang on, kid.

He must be so scared. Once, when Mickey and I were out, we hit a tree, bent the skid and were thrown off the machine. Mickey fractured his wrist, and I was afraid to leave him in the snow.

Maybe it was the reason why I didn't want him tagging after me. I hated being responsible for his welfare.

No. Actually I hated failing.

There should be fireworks bursting because with a shout and an aha in my brain I realize why I'm in this mess.

And I won't fail. Not this time.

The snow kicks up behind me, the machine vibrating as I cut off the road and down toward Sixmile. Here, the forest grows around me, poplar and pine trees, icy-laced brush. My headlight carves out an almost snow-covered track.

Yes.

Sixmile is little more than an overgrown, weedy trickle of water, mostly marsh, jammed with dead logs and broken trees.

My machine sinks into the softer ground, so I gun it, following the barest of trek indentations out onto the greater lake.

Here, the world is vast and dark, and as I open it up, the wind has swept his trail.

"Leo!"

My voice is nothing in the gust of the wind. Stopping the machine, my heart slams into my ribs as a cloud of snow settles around me.

All is quiet, save for the low rumble of the sled. A pristine moon above casts a glow across the ice.

Rumples in the surface evidence a quick frost—ducks or geese caught in the ripple of ice, and snow blows across the surface.

The cold settles inside me, as if I've been outrunning it and it's found my bones, brutal and haunting.

"Leo!"

My voice falls back to me, the darkness formidable. I see my breath, a crystalline puff, another, and I pull up my scarf.

The wind moans through the willow trees at shore.

Then I hear it. A voice.

Rem!

It's more of a moan than a name. I still.

That's when I spot the hole that has opened in the lake, near the shore.

Rafting. It's when the wind pushes ice sheets over themselves—especially near shore and breaks the ice open at pressure ridges.

The wind gets in and stirs the warmer water to the surface, thawing the ice from within.

My chest tightens. No.

189

I drive to shore and skirt my sled along the shallow until I see it, some forty feet out, glistening and dark, like oil under pale light.

"No!"

I know I turn stupid, but what would you do? Gone are the reminders, the lessons learned by every grade schooler in the north about broken ice. I scramble out to the hole, drop to my knees and crawl to the side.

The hole is large—big enough for a sled to fall through and I stare into it, unable to breathe.

"Leo!" I know I'm screaming but I can't stop. Could you?

I sit back, breathing hard. No, this isn't right.

This is Not. Right.

Then I hear a crack. It's bright and sharp against the night and I look down. A fissure has opened between my knees.

You've got to be kidding me.

I scamper back, then get up, and the cracking sharpens behind me. My boots slip, I trip, and at my feet, the ice opens.

Not like this.

I'm running. Full out, toward shore, slipping on the ice, the ice heaving behind me. And, I'm yelling. I don't know what, just a shout, more horror than fear, really but—

My feet betray me, and I fall, slamming into the ice, the air exploding out of me. I roll and stare at the sky like a walleye on land, gulping.

The ice cracks stop no more than a foot away, and I lay, paralyzed.

If I move, the frigid depths will swallow me, and it will be over.

It seems right, doesn't it? That after everything, I end up like Mickey, at the bottom of a lake.

Probably, really, I deserve it.

I close my eyes, waiting for the darkness to take me, because I have nothing. No air, no strength, no...

Hope.

And, of course, in that moment, it's not Eve, or Booker, or Burke or even my father in my head, but a stranger I met just twelve hours ago. *Have you ever considered that maybe, you're just running from yourself?*

I close my eyes, and I'm an idiot because, yes.

Stupidly, yes.

And now my eyes are frozen because Mark is right.

This hasn't been about my cold cases or saving Eve or even becoming a cop again.

I can't live with the fact that I didn't turn around. That I didn't want my brother with me. That I peddled ahead on the road.

And stop telling me about forgiveness because I have none for a guy who ditched his brother to die.

Overhead a flush of birds lift, as if startled.

It's just me, and moon.

And, apparently, Mark.

What if we reached out to our Higher Power instead?

My throat is thick, my body heavy and I can't move, pinned as it were, to my grave.

The thought leads me back to today's meeting. To the crucifix and the plaque on the wall I read walking into the church.

If we confess our sins, he is faithful and just, and will forgive our sins and cleanse us from all unrighteousness.

The words stay, latch on, seep in, like heat.

What if my forgiveness doesn't have to come from, well, me? Because, of course I don't have the ability to forgive myself.

Who could?

But maybe that's the point. Maybe it's *always* been beyond

me.

I hear Art's voice. *"So the question is…who gave you the watch?"*

Huh. Maybe God has been at the helm of the journey all along.

After all, he is the Lord of Time.

Trusting that He will make all things right…if I surrender…

Maybe you don't think I have anything to ask forgiveness for, but you're not lying here, frozen.

And you haven't dreamed of your brother, disappearing, trying to rewrite the ending of that nightmare, over and over for the last fifteen years.

So yes, I close my eyes, put my hand over my face. *I'm so sorry. I can't do this. I'm done running.*

And, although it takes everything inside me, *save me.*

I open my eyes, aware of the wetness that is freezing on my face and stare at the stars, winking down.

One unlatches and falls.

I'm aware, now of my breathing, as if I'm coming back to myself and I sit up, and stare at the hole in the ice.

Oh, God. How do I tell—

"Rembrandt!"

The voice calls again, and I still, testing the wind.

"Rembrandt!" So, not God—I know, but I'm a writer, too. I have a vivid imagination—but a *real* voice sounds from the shore and I turn to my knees, scramble up.

The ice cracks again, but I'm fast and I fling myself to shore, following my name.

"Leo!" My voice carries now, and I listen. And hear the call again, this time fainter.

It's coming from the woods, and I pull out my phone, and flick on the light, pushing through the snowy bramble.

Then I see it—a deer blind, or at least the wreck of one, with three dilapidated wooden sides and a fraying roof. And inside, shivering and curled in a ball is my nine-year old brother.

I would have missed him if I hadn't fallen long enough for the air to clear. For me to hear.

"Bro, what happened?"

He's shivering so hard he can't speak. This is a good sign—if he weren't he'd be further along the hypothermic chain. I take off my gloves and feel his clothing. He's wearing insulated pants and his legs are wet, but not much above his waist.

"Did you fall in?"

He nods, his entire body lurching with the effort.

"Okay, we'll get you home." I reach to help him up and he shouts.

"What—?"

He leans back, moaning, and I look him over, touching his arms, then his legs. When I get to his right ankle, he jerks.

"Did you sprain it?"

"Maybe." He's whimpering now and explanations can wait.

I need to get him warm before he freezes. So, I climb into the blind, put my legs and arms around him. Unzipping his jacket, I pull it off him, then turn it around and push his arms back into his jacket, the front to the back. Then, I unzip my jacket and my coveralls and pull him against the heat of my skin.

He sags against me as I zip us back up, in my coat.

Good thing our dad is bigger than both of us.

Then, I pull out my phone.

My mother picks up on the second ring, probably camped out by the land line on the wall.

"I found him."

Her gasp is so loud, I hear it in my soul. Then, "Is he alive?"

193

"Yes. He's hurt, though, and cold, so I need SAR to come to me. Go to the boat launch on Parley Lake. I'll bring him there."

"Oh, Rem…" Her breath hitches. "Thank you. Thank you for finding your brother."

Those are the words I've waited to hear my entire life.

She wanted to bring him home.

CHAPTER 18

Eve cradled her cup of coffee as the ER doc finished taking Rembrandt's blood pressure, pretty sure his injuries were fresh.

She wanted to tell the doc, a woman in her mid-forties, that this was Rembrandt's standard appearance. Okay, yes, maybe he was a *smidgen* more beat up—the bump on his head had turned an eerie green, and his shoulder was deeply bruised—but yes, Rembrandt came prepackaged with a tendency toward trouble.

And saving lives.

She just hoped she could keep up.

She'd driven Dottie Stone to the hospital to meet Vince and the Waconia SAR crew.

Wept, right along with his mother when Rembrandt showed up, carrying his brother against him, the boy's arms locked around his neck.

Sheesh, the man knew how to do hero. Even with his matted hair and his bruised body. He'd stripped down to his jeans for the exam, making a face at the flimsy gown the tech gave him.

Oh, he was a fine specimen of a man, and she just stood in the hallway like a gawker as the doc cleared him.

"Told you," Rem said as he hopped off the table and grabbed his shirt. He pulled it back on, then spotted her looking at him, and she smiled, lifted a shoulder.

Yeah, she wanted very much to take this man home.

He grinned at her, something sweet in his eyes, a look she'd never really seen before.

In fact, despite his bruises, he seemed different. Especially as he came out into the hall, took the coffee from her, set it down on a nearby bed table, then backed her right up against the wall. Braced his hand over her shoulder. "You like what you see?"

She pressed her hand to his chest. "Mmmhmm."

He ran his other hand under her chin, lifted her face to his, met her eyes.

And then he kissed her.

She knew Rembrandt could kiss, knew that he could steal her very name from her, but this was different, too.

Nothing of hurry. Or urgency. Or even desperation.

Nothing of pain, or regret or sometimes even fear.

This was a kiss that spoke of happy endings, of lingering and belonging.

Of home.

She wound her arms around him and pulled him close, wanting every inch of him.

Maybe he felt the same because he curled his arm around her shoulders and deepened his kiss.

"Ahem."

The voice was deep, a man, but Rembrandt didn't jerk away. He slowly finished his kiss, then lifted his head. Looked down the hall.

"In the middle of something, Dad."

Vincent Stone stood still wearing his stocking cap, his jeans and boots, although he'd shed his jacket, leaving his thermal long sleeve shirt. "I see that." He smiled, shook his head. "Your brother wants to talk to you."

Rem made a sound deep in his chest, but stepped away and took her hand. "Of course."

They followed his father down a corridor, then up the elevator and down another hallway to an interior room.

The bed swallowed little Leo, but he sat propped up with pillows, his dark hair askew, his leg in a cast, an IV in his arm.

"Hey, little buddy," Rembrandt said. He let Eve go and walked over to Leo and tousled his hair. "You're a real toughie."

Dottie sat in a chair nearby, looking at Rembrandt like he might be a superhero.

"How'd it happen?" Rembrandt asked.

"I don't know. I was driving, and then in a flash, the ice broke and the sled went in and I fell off. I think one of the skids landed on my leg."

"Ouch."

Eve was watching Dottie's face, the way she tightened her jaw, drew in a breath.

"The sled nearly pulled me under, but it broke free and then I crawled to shore."

"Good job." Rembrandt sat on the bed. "I'll bet you were pretty scared."

Leo lifted a shoulder, and the action was so Rembrandt-like Eve wanted to laugh. "I kept thinking about what you said. You know, when you were scared?"

"What was that?"

"You can either run, or you can face it."

"I said that, huh?"

Leo nodded, then looked away, curling the bedsheets between

his fists. "Thanks for coming after me."

Rem took a breath, closed his eyes. Then he opened them and nodded. "That's what brothers are for, kiddo." He got up, leaned down and kissed Leo's forehead.

And shoot, Eve wanted to cry.

"Let's get you home," she said and took Rembrandt's hand.

Rem said goodbye to his parents and let her lead him down the hallway.

"Home?" he asked as they took the elevator down.

"Home," she said, and he pulled her against him again.

The night was crisp, her breath forming tiny puffs as they walked out to the Jeep. She got in the driver's side, and he handed her the keys.

Then he leaned back in the seat and closed his eyes.

As she studied his face a realization swept over her. She was still alive. Gene Latsky hadn't found her, hadn't abducted her, hadn't strangled her and left her in the trunk of the car that had killed Julia.

And tomorrow, she was going to help Rem construct a case against Latsky that would put him in prison for the rest of his life.

His phone buzzed in the pocket between their seats as she stopped at a light. She picked it up and read a text from Shelby.

>>*On my way to pick up Daggert.*

Which meant, her Rem, old Rem, the one who loved her more than his life, would leave, soon.

And young Rem, the one she would grow old with, would remain.

She pulled into her driveway, the moon high overhead, the stars winking down. Rem sat with his eyes closed, his lashes dark against his cheeks, so painfully handsome, she almost didn't want to wake him.

Probably a bad idea, because inviting him inside would only lead to more of the way he kissed her.

And she had no intention of sending him on his way.

But, for five lifetimes, he'd come searching for her, trying to save her—them—because they *belonged* together.

If she could, she'd marry him tonight, right now.

"Rem?" She put her hand on his shoulder. "Are you awake?"

He roused, and breathed in deep, as if clawing his way through darkness. Looked over at her.

And for a moment, she thought he—old Rem with the wise eyes and resonance to his words—was already gone. But then he smiled. "Someday we can wake up together."

Indeed.

"Let's make a fire. Get you warm," she said, and he made a sound of agreement.

She got out and headed to the door. Rembrandt crunched his way up the walk behind her. Getting out her keys, she climbed onto her porch just as Rembrandt's phone rang.

She fit her key into the lock, turning as he picked it up.

"Burke—"

And he hadn't realized she'd been holding her breath.

It was over.

She opened her door, pushed inside and pulled off her scarf.

But Rem had caught the door with his foot— "What?"

She stilled, turned.

Rem's eyes widened, and he stared at her. "Eve—"

"You're just in time," said a voice behind her. Then a hand clamped over her mouth.

Rem dropped the phone. "Let her go!" He followed her in, but the man pulled her back, pressed a knife to her neck.

Rem put up his hands, stopped his advance. Behind him, the

storm door softly closed. "Please, Gene, let her go."

"Funny. You said the same thing to me earlier tonight. And I had no idea what you were talking about. Until, then I did. So I went for a drive, out to have a visit with my old pal, Leo, and found that you were there first."

"This is between you and me—"

"I don't know how you figured it out so fast. When you showed up at the bar in Montrose, I thought for sure you were there for me."

Rem drew in a breath.

Gene had dragged her back, toward her kitchen, his hand around her neck, squeezing out her breath.

She tensed, fighting the gorge of panic.

Think, Eve.

She'd had training. She knew how to fight. Hadn't Rem told her that she'd struggled?

She made a fist and swung it down, hard, and nailed Gene in the softs.

He grunted enough to jerk away.

She turned and grabbed his knife hand, pressing it away from her.

Slammed her palm into his nose.

He shouted and blood spurted.

That's right you—

He slapped her. Pain exploded across her face, turned her.

As she hit the wall, through the strobe of her vision, she saw Rembrandt, already flying through the air.

They went down with a crash in her kitchen. Rembrandt punched him, and Gene grunted. Again.

But Gene had picked up one of the pieces of firewood near her door and slammed it against Rem's damaged shoulder.

His pain sounded through the house as he staggered backward.

Gene brought the wood down again, and she thought she heard bones break.

Rem howled, but it turned into a roar as he rolled over, his arm dangling and kicked at Gene.

Gene took a swipe at his head, but Rem ducked and the log slammed into the floor. He scrambled backwards as Gene advanced on him, still swinging.

He was going to connect, and soon, and Rem would die.

No. *No—*

Eve braced her hand on the wall, grit her teeth. She tasted blood but forced herself to her feet.

Used the wall to slip into the kitchen.

Then, while Gene was stepping up to bat, she eased open a drawer at the end of her counter and pulled out her police-issue Glock.

Not without her resources.

"Drop it, Gene. Or I promise you, I will shoot you."

He turned and stared at Eve. Ground his jaw.

And gave her the look of a man who could assault and strangle thirty-eight women.

Kill a four-year-old girl.

And murder a woman he knew as a friend.

His eyes narrowed, turned dark and he called her a word that confirmed who he was.

Rem pulled himself up to a chair, and she wanted to wince at his arm, but she didn't take her eyes from Gene.

He still held the wood in his grip.

And then, he laughed. "Do you really think, honey, that you're going to stop me when the famous Rembrandt Stone couldn't?"

So Rem was right. This *was* a game.

He took a step toward her.

"Stop, Gene."

"Shoot me." He took another step.

"Shoot him, Eve," Rembrandt said, breathing hard.

She looked at Gene, tightened her jaw.

"Shoot him!"

Gene lifted the log, as if to swing it.

She pulled the trigger.

His blow, however, hit her just as the gun went off, and knocked it from her hands. It went spinning away.

He grabbed her by the neck and slammed her against the wall. His grip tightened, his face inches from hers. "I don't know. Do I kill you first, and make him watch, or does he die knowing what I'm going to do to you?"

She clawed at his face.

He hit her so hard she might have blacked out a moment.

She woke to a death struggle for the gun between Rem and Gene. Rembrandt bled from a cut on his face. Gene's blood saturated his shirt. The grunts were deep, the grappling lethal. Rem's arm viced Gene's neck, his legs around him. Gene pummeled his body.

She screamed. "Rem!"

The knife. If she could find the knife—

She pushed herself off the floor, but the room turned to sharp angles.

"Run, Eve!" Rem shouted.

She moved toward the back door, if she could just—

With a shout, Gene landed a fist into Rem so hard it unlatched Rem's hold. He writhed on the floor, his ribs probably broken.

Gene got up, breathing hard, his face washed with blood, something out of a slasher film, and aimed the gun at Rem, breathing hard.

"Game over," he said. "Tonight, you die."

The shot deafened her, and she screamed, curling into a ball, and kept screaming. *Rembrandt!*

She couldn't stop. Even after the silence.

Then, "Eve! *Eve! Stop!*"

The voice cut through her screaming, and she pulled her hands from her head.

Rembrandt knelt next to her, his face torn, his mouth bleeding, but—alive.

What—?

He pulled her up. "It's okay. I'm okay."

"No—I saw him—I heard—"

"Rembrandt Stone doesn't die this time around." The voice came from John Booker, who stood at the edge of her kitchen, holding his weapon.

She looked at Gene. He lay in a puddle of his own blood on her recently remodeled tile floor.

What?

"And neither does Eve Mulligan."

She looked at Booker. "What?" His words rushed over her. "Did this happen *before?*"

He sighed, then looked at Rem.

"Don't answer that, Booker," Rem said.

Sirens sounded outside, but she ran her hands over Rem, touched his shoulder, his head. She grabbed a towel, cast on the floor nearby and pressed it to his wound.

"You're not so pretty yourself," Rem said, and gave her a weak grin, his fingers going to the deepening bruise on his face.

Then, he pulled her to himself.

And the bravest man she knew quietly fell apart in her arms.

She held him and wept, too. "I love you, Rem. I love you."

He finally leaned back, his eyes widening, his breath catching. "Eve—"

And she knew.

Just *knew.*

"No, not yet, no—"

He took her face in his hands. "Eve. I'll be right here. Now, and then. I will always be here."

"Rem—"

Then he kissed her. And this time his touch was hard, desperate, holding on. Never letting go.

She lost him then—she knew it, and yet, found him, too, because the man who released her met her eyes, something solid and purposeful and true in them.

And when he smiled, she did too.

I know what you're thinking.

CHAPTER 19

Rem, you got your hide handed to you.

Yep. Pretty much.

But maybe that's the way of it. You give it your best, and hope for help.

At least, I think that's how it works from now on.

Booker's words are ringing in my head as the locomotive of time rushes me back to the present. *"Rembrandt Stone doesn't die this time around."*

He went back to save my life. This thought has me undone as I land on all fours on a tile floor.

The feel of Eve is still in my hands, the taste of her in my mouth.

I touch my forehead to the floor a moment before I open my eyes, maybe in prayer because I utter a quiet, *please.*

And that's when the shouting starts.

"Clear the room!"

A voice behind me speaks, and it's a familiar voice, although I don't place it. But it comes to me quickly that I'm in police head-quarters, in the rotunda where I left.

Where a biological bomb had just exploded. I lift my head, and get a quick lay of the land.

A wedding, given the settings on the tables, the bride and groom—still Mariana and Booker—standing on the landing between stairs, police officers pushing other guests back, away from... me.

I'm still crouched next to the statue of Neptune, in the center of the room, my hands pressed to the tile floor, near a fallen display of flowers.

How can it be that I didn't change *anything*? That I'm back in the exact situation I left.

Except, back then my lungs were closing, a paralysis overtaking my body.

I check. I can breathe. Or maybe not because as I look up and survey the room, I see him—a man standing on the other side of the room, dressed in a tuxedo, holding a detonator in his left hand, his thumb on a dead man's switch.

And I know him.

Ramses Vega, now forty-something, aged twenty-three years. His former handsome dark-haired visage is marred by the tough times he saw in Stillwater Prison. He's built, less of the wiry soccer player he was, but more bulk, like he did a few push-ups in his cell. Again, like before, I wonder how he got out, but maybe it doesn't matter.

Only that he's here, at his mother's wedding, about to detonate a bomb.

Why am I not surprised?

He's backing toward the entrance to the room—the front doors, holding down the toggle, and now I know why I'm crouching behind Neptune.

He can't see me. His back is to me as he sneaks out.

Then, to confirm, a voice threads into my ears. "Are you in place, Rem?"

It's a female voice, and I realize I'm wearing ear pods. Not the security kind but attached by Bluetooth to my phone.

I'm on a call. And the voice on the other end is my former partner, Shelby.

Ready for what? I want to ask, but it's not hard to figure out.

"Give him a couple more steps," Shelby says. Then, quietly, "Are you sure you can do this?"

Do *what*? But I'm doing the math and my guess is they want me to take him out.

Except, what if his thumb moves off the switch? My logical guess is, *ka-boom.*

Why, Ramses? But maybe I can guess.

In my original history with Mariana, she ran for mayor in my district with no mention of her son, Ramses, from Brazil. I figured it was because he'd been killed by his own bomb at CityPerk.

What if it was simpler—she didn't want the world to know she had a son?

Why?

Eve and I figured that Ramses Vega bombed the coffee shops in protest of the slave labor used to grow the organic Green Earth coffee from his home country, in Brazil.

More, Vega is the daughter of a wealthy group of coffee lords.

It's possible they used Ramses to pull her strings. Even in prison. A foothold into our city, via our mayor.

Wouldn't be the first time the mafia tried to put someone into political power.

Maybe she got Ramses out so she could cut the strings. I glance at her. Out of all the people Booker would choose, Mariana wouldn't even make the list.

But Booker is smart. He's not going to be snowed by a beautiful woman.

And this woman now has her hands to her face, crying, Booker's arms around her.

Maybe this is Ramses' last act of freedom. Or vengeance. Or he's simply a pawn—I don't know.

But I do care. So, "Yes," I whisper. "I can do this."

And by *this*, I mean tackle Vega after he takes two more steps, keep my hand on the dead man switch and hold him down long enough for the cavalry to jump in.

"On three—" says Shelby.

"No," I growl. "On me."

I crouch and take a breath. It's only now that I notice I'm wearing a tux, too. So, I'm not an undercover thug anymore—that's an improvement.

Still, if this goes south, I don't know what I'll be sacrificing.

Does it matter? I think too much. Just do the right thing—something I learned on the journey. Let go and trust. Another thing. And most of all—

Stop trying to fix the future.

Ramses takes another step, and he's nearly to me.

"Please don't die," Shelby says, and I smile.

Yes, Shelby.

He moves, and I launch. There's some finesse to my move because I aim for his hand first, grabbing it and tightening his hold on the dead man's switch. The other arm I put around his neck, holding him.

Then I kick out his feet and down we go.

We land hard, me on top of him, and he's writhing, screaming.

"Hurry up!" I shout, not sure how much longer I can hold his grip down.

Shouts, and chairs tip over and suddenly hands are on us. Ramses is struggling, but another hand goes over mine to secure the switch.

Ramses' fist slams into my face, a glancing blow that rings my bell. But I hang on.

The grip over mine is secure, so I tuck my legs around Ramses and we roll over to the side.

But in his struggles, he's grabbed a knife—not sure where he got that, and he slashes at the other hand before someone else grabs his knife hand by the wrist and pins it to the floor.

"Give it up," says the voice.

I recognize Burke's baritone, as he disarms Ramses. He too is wearing a tux, and glances at me, his face grim, shaking his head. "Always have to be the hero."

I smile. Burke's again bald, age in his eyes, but he's alive, and *here* so I must have done at least one thing right.

Ramses is trying to let go of the trigger, but I have his hand in a vise, and my assistant, a young man in his mid-thirties, with dark hair, and also wearing a suit, has both hands on his grip.

"Find the bomb," I say. "We need to disarm it."

"Already on it," says Shelby in my ear. I'm surprised the pod hasn't fallen out with the struggle.

"Make it snappy!"

My dark-haired helper smiles.

The room has been cleared, and it's Burke and me and our friend holding Ramses down as a man in full-bomb protection walks into my view. He goes over to the planter where I found the bio bomb and pulls from it a canister.

He sets it on the table. As if he's going to disarm it.

Here?

"Hey—get that thing out of here!" I shout.

"It's on a dead man switch," Shelby says. "It's activated. If we break the signal, even by removing it, it will go off."

That's why Ramses was running. To cut the signal. And, I suppose, to live another day.

"Sit tight. Lenny is good at his job."

Lenny. I glance at the man who has taken off the casing of the bomb and is peering inside.

What? You've got to be kidding me.

It *can't* be.

He lays out a pouch of tools, even as Ramses is shouting his fury. The EOD guy pulls from the pouch some tweezers and a snipper.

Please, let him get this right.

I close my eyes and think about the last moments with Eve. The phone call from Burke on the porch—

"Burke."

Admittedly, I was still trying to orient myself after falling asleep in the Jeep, then walking up Eve's driveway. I felt frozen to my core, but warming fast when I thought of taking Eve in my arms by her fire.

"He's in the wind, Rem. I can't find him."

Burke's words to me just as Eve unlocked her door and stepped inside.

And I knew—even before I shouted—that Gene would be waiting.

That he'd grab her and try and kill her while I watched.

He should have known Eve better. That she'd fight back. But when he hit her, I stopped thinking.

I'm not sure how he ended up with the gun pointed at me. I remember my shouting at Eve to shoot him, remember her pulling the trigger.

Then she was down and Gene was on top of me.

I dislocated my shoulder during the fight. And when he backed away from me with the weapon, I knew.

This time around I wouldn't come back to myself. The journey would end, right then, in Eve's kitchen. And after he killed me, he'd kill Eve.

So I braced myself. And prayed. Because what else does a man have at the end of his life but a prayer?

Gene's body shook with the force of a bullet to the back of the head. Then he dropped hard.

And I wasn't dead.

But John Booker stood in the kitchen, his gun still hot and I looked at him and, in my soul, knew, he was not the John Booker of then, but of now.

He'd used the watch to go back in time and save me.

Maybe it was something I said.

Ramses is still shouting when I hear Shelby in my ear— "It's over. You can let go."

I glance at the EOD expert, who is now placing the deactivated bomb into a bomb-proof container. He gives me a thumbs up.

"Let go," I say to my assistant, who nods and steps back. Then I let go too, roll Ramses over and put my knee in his back to keep him down.

Burke takes one of Ramses arms. My assistant has the other.

A uniform comes in to cuff him and I get off and walk away.

Brace my hand on a nearby table.

Maybe I don't die today, either.

The EOD guy has taken off his helmet, and now shakes out his blond hair. Sweat has beaded along his brow, and for a moment, I can't move.

Leo Fitzgerald. He grins at me. "Good job, Inspector."

Huh.

Then he removes the case.

The officer has Ramses on his feet and is leading him away, and I brace the other hand on the table, my body oddly shaking.

"Bro, you okay?"

I look over and my assistant comes to me. He's holding a cloth napkin over the wound Ramses slashed into his hand. "I don't know how you always manage to be in the right place at the right time."

He's got dark hair, blue eyes, is lean and fit and reminds me of a face I saw in the mirror once upon a time. "Leo?"

He raises his eyebrows. "How hard did he hit you?"

Leo. My *brother.*

I stare at him, trying to form words.

"You doing all right, bro?"

And I don't know why, but I want to weep. Clearly, I'm tired, strung out and ready to just…go home.

Home.

"Rem!"

The voice is sweet and hot and slides through me, latches on and for a moment, I can't move.

Eve?

I turn, and there she is, running around the tables toward me. She wears a pale orange dress, heels and has her red hair up in a messy bun. Her hazel-green eyes fix on mine, so much love, so much relief in her gaze that I open my mouth to catch another breath.

Then she flings her arms around me, her body pressed up to mine, and she's holding me so tight I can't breathe and I don't care.

She's still mine.

"I'm okay, babe. I'm okay," I say.

But she's crying a little, kissing my neck, then she leans back and kisses me, hard, possessive, just a little desperate.

And it reminds me of the kiss I gave her right before I left her in the past.

I'm going to be honest and say I wasn't sure I'd ever see her again. Were you?

She pulls away, and her mascara is smudged, so I run a thumb across her cheek. "I told you. I'll be right here. Always."

She blinks at me then, frowns, then nods, smiling again. "Yes. Yes, you did."

Her hand finds mine, and Burke walks over, clamps me on the shoulder. "Fast thinking, Rem. How did you see him?"

Uh, I don't know. Was he a waiter, or part of the party? So, "Just a hunch."

He shakes his head and gives a half chuckle. "Right. Of course."

"Rembrandt Stone, one of these days you're going to give me a heart attack." Shelby has walked into the crowd, which is now being cordoned off by police tape. Silas is directing traffic not far away, dressed in his fancy duds like the rest of us.

Apparently, the wedding of the year.

Shelby has cut her hair, but not as short as it was in Miami, in my last life. Not far away, I spot the teenager who just got her license, Daphne. She's wearing a sundress, her golden hair in corn-rows.

"Chief," I say, taking a chance.

"And don't you forget that," Shelby says, pulling the pod from my ear, and putting it in my hand.

I laugh, but inside, my brain is starting to catch up.

It worked. It actually worked.

Gene Latsky *didn't* kill thirty-eight women, Burke isn't blind, Shelby is still the chief, and...and Eve is holding my hand.

High five for, well, team fate, maybe.

"It's a good thing Booker and Mariana finished their vows before all the excitement happened," Leo says. He lifts a hand to someone behind me and I turn.

Frankie and Zeke are standing behind the yellow tape, holding hands. Zeke is wearing a hard look, and I wonder if he's wishing he had gotten into the scuffle. If I know Zeke—and I do, because he's my protégé—Frankie probably had to keep a grip on him as we wrestled Ramses.

They wave at us and I wave back.

"C'mon, Batman. Let's get home," Eve says, pulling on me. "Enough excitement for one day."

"He needs to give a statement," Shelby says.

"Later, Shelbs," Eve says, clearly pulling rank.

As my wife.

On the way out, I look over and Booker meets my eyes. His arms are still around Mariana. Not a great day for them.

But I nod at him, and smile.

He nods back.

I wonder if he knows. Two to one odds he does.

We walk out of the building toward the parking garage and I fish into my pocket for my keys.

Good thing I'm a creature of habit. I click the fob, looking for the car. I'm expecting my wife's pedestrian Ford Escape.

Not a spiffy Porsche 911 Carrera 4 convertible. I stop, stare at it, a sudden fist in my gut. The licenses plate reads, STLWRT.

"Where did I…" And I know I'm giving myself away, but this is Eve. She knows. "Eve, where did I get this?"

She stops, looks at me. "Oh." Then she looks at the car. "You bought it at auction, after you and Burke impounded it. It belonged to a Russian mobster you took down not long ago."

"Alexander Malakov."

"Yes. He had a brother that Booker put away years ago. You worked that man's son to take down the organization."

So, Burke turned Boris's son into an informant.

Slick.

I slide into the cool embrace of my wheels and press the ignition button.

Of course, a classic song fills the speakers.

"Fortunate Son," by Creedence.

I lower the top and pull out of the parking lot as Eve toes off her shoes.

I love my life.

CHAPTER 20

The realization slides over me as we drive through Minneapolis, and I'm taking another chance, but my gut says we still live in the half-remodeled craftsman on Drew Avenue.

I don't expect anything more. Really. This is enough.

Okay, I'm not being *quite* honest. You know what I want.

But I'm still not in the habit of hoping.

Although, for a moment I'm back on the ice, feeling the heat flush through me. Hope. I can't deny the fact that it's starting to reawaken in my chest.

Eve takes my hand over the console as we cut down our street. "The Boys of Summer," is playing, and she says, "Maybe tomorrow we should go to my parents' house, go swimming."

I glance at her. "Or tonight." I wink.

She blushes. "I'll have to think about that."

C'mon, she's not going to turn me down, is she?

We pull into the driveway.

The house has been freshly painted a light gray, the trim white, the shutters black. A pot of geraniums sits at the top of the stairs to the deck.

I park in the driveway, get out and follow Eve up the stairs. Pause at the top.

Across the street, I spot Gia leaving her house. She has a kid on her hip, and Alex pulls the door shut behind her. He spots me and waves.

I wave back.

A million tiny things that change lives in a thousand minuscule ways.

Eve has opened the door and I walk in behind her.

The house is as I remember it. A large sofa in the front room with a flat screen television. My office to the right, the worn leather chair in the corner.

There is no box of cold case files on the floor. I can't decide if it's relief I feel, or sorrow.

Wait. Yes, I can. Definitely relief. I so hope I've kept my promise to Eve to stop traveling.

The smell of baking cookies drifts out from the kitchen, sweeps through me and it's so familiar my stomach drops.

"So, how was the wedding?" My mom comes from the kitchen, wiping her hands from the towel.

"Are those cookies?" Eve says as she dumps her shoes, her purse on a bench by the door. "You spoil us, Dottie."

"What are grandmas for?"

I still. *Grandmas?*

I can't breathe.

"Where is she?" Eve asks, and heads down the hallway toward the kitchen.

"Outside, with Vince," my mother says, as if she hasn't tilted my world sideways. She pats my cheek. "Ashley is more like you every day."

Time stops.

I'm not crying. Are you crying?

My throat is thick as I walk to the kitchen.

Eve is outside on the deck, letting down her hair, laughing as she waves to a little girl on a swing. Behind her, my father, dressed in a pair of jeans and a T-shirt, pushes her.

But my eyes are on the little girl. She has blonde hair, and it's in braids—a touch from her grandma, I'll bet. She wears a dress and tennis shoes, but her knees are scuffed.

I press my hands to my temples.

Then my father grabs her, wraps her up in his arms, and she squeals in laughter.

I am undone.

Behind me, my mother is taking cookies out of the oven. "By the way, a box of books came."

Books? I turn. "What books?"

"Yours."

"Mine?"

My mom laughs. "Yes. Yours. Your new time-travel novel. I put the box on your desk."

Are you kidding me? I didn't, did I?

Then it hits me. It's real.

Oh, thank you, God. This is my life.

This is *My. Life.*

My mom sets the pan of cookies on a cutting board on the counter. "I don't know how you find the time to write. But I can't wait to read it."

Yeah, me too. But I have a feeling I know the plot.

I walk out to the deck, the sunshine warm on my skin, and notice the big elm is gone.

"Daddy!" My daughter wiggles out of my father's grip, and my knees buckle on their own as I kneel to catch her.

She races into my embrace, her arms around me, and I'm not sure what I've done to deserve such a greeting, but I don't care. *Ashley.*

I am trying not to crush her, not to break out in more tears and make a fool out of myself. I close my eyes and breathe in the cottony softness of her, feel her smooth skin on my rough face, and lose myself in the embrace of unconditional love.

I get a lot of things wrong. And most of the time I hate it. But this time I don't.

There is such thing as a happy ending.

"Anyone want a cookie?" My mother breaks off the reunion too soon, but it's okay. I'm not going anywhere.

Ever again.

Ashley scampers to the table to nab a cookie. My father steps up to the deck, too, glancing at me.

"You okay, son?"

I run a thumb under my eye and nod.

But nothing escapes Eve. She walks over. Threads her fingers through mine and draws me away. "Rem?" she says softly. "Did you just get here?"

I look at her, and her gaze fixes on mine with a knowing look.

"Yeah, I did. Back at the wedding. Right before I jumped Ramses."

"Where were you?"

She knows the right question, doesn't she?

"In your kitchen. Right after Booker killed Gene."

Her mouth slowly opens, then. "Yes, that would be right." And then she smiles. "You're *here.*"

I nod.

"Except, you missed it all." Her expression turns wistful.

I glance past her, at the space where the massive elm sat.

Growing in its place is a smaller, ten-foot maple. And for a moment, I see Ashley and Eve helping me lower it to the ground, a family affair. It's just a split-second flash, but...it's a memory.

Like before, when I landed in time and the current memories folded over the last ones.

"No," I say. "I didn't miss it. Really. Just give me time."

She frames my face with her hands. "That's what we have, Rem. Time."

"Daddy! Do you want a cookie?" Ashley is handing me a cookie in her grubby paw. She grins up at me, and my gaze lands to the scar on her forehead.

Another memory surfaces, the one of us in the ER after she hit her head on a pipe at the zoo. She's clutching Gomer, her lost teddy bear.

He's bloody, a casualty of the event.

I crouch before her. "Ash. Is Gomer still missing?"

She goes somber, her tiny lip a pout. "Mmmhmm."

I smile. "Wait here."

Eve is frowning at me as I get up and head inside, to our laundry room.

It's off the kitchen, small and tidy. A few towels sit in a basket, waiting to be washed. On the top of the dryer, folded, are a couple of Ashley's dresses, a pair of shorts, a T-shirt.

No bear.

But I have a suddenly distinct memory of washing that bear, along with her clothes, after we got home from the ER.

I look inside the dryer—not there.

As I'm turning to go, however, I see a spot of fur on the floor, wedged between the dryer and the wall.

Gomer. I pull him out. He's tired and worn, his eye is missing, the product of much love. Stupid, beautiful bear.

I bring him out to Ashley, whose eyes widen. "You found him! Daddy!"

She grabs the bear and clutches him to herself.

"Yes, well, your father is a detective," Eve says, shaking her head, her eyes rolling.

Yes, yes, I am.

I grab a cookie and put my arm around Eve. Look at the backyard, at the swing set I made. At the glorious blue sky. Listen to my parents chatting about their home in Florida. Ashley giggles as she sits on my father's lap. ww

This is my world.

Be stalwart. The word settles through me.

The motto of a former time-traveler.

Then I turn to Eve and say, with love in my voice, "I think we should get a boat."

THE TRUE LIES
OF REMBRANDT STONE

Dear Reader,

We've reached the end of Rembrandt's adventures (or have we?) and want to offer you the deepest gratitude for taking this journey with us.

We hope you enjoyed reading or listening to Rem's stories as we did creating them.

From the beginning, our desire was to write a series that offered a perspective on wrestling with regret, and would explore the idea of forgiving the person in our lives often the hardest to forgive; ourselves. And that there is a Person beyond us that longs to bring us fully into an understanding of that kind of forgiveness.

And while each of us had a crucial role in creating The True Lies of Rembrandt Stone, it was Susie's vision, passion, and leadership that brought Rembrandt to life.

To you and your own journey of hope and restoration,

Susie, Jim, and *David*

"Blessed is the man who remains steadfast under trial, for when he has stood the test he will receive the crown of life, which God has promised to those who love him." - James 1:12

Meet
David James Warren

Susan May Warren is the USA Today bestselling, Christy and RITA award–winning author of more than eighty novels whose compelling plots and unforgettable characters have won acclaim with readers and reviewers alike. The mother of four grown children, and married to her real-life hero for over 30 years, she loves travelling and telling stories about life, adventure and faith.

For exciting updates on her new releases, previous books, and more, visit her website at www.susanmaywarren.com.

James L. Rubart is 28 years old, but lives trapped inside an older man's body. He's the best-selling, Christy Hall of Fame author of ten novels and loves to send readers on mind-bending journeys they'll remember months after they finish one of his stories. He's dad to the two most outstanding sons on the planet and lives with his amazing wife on a small lake in eastern Washington.

More at www.jameslrubart.com

David Curtis Warren is making his literary debut in these novels, and he's never been more excited. He looks forward to creating more riveting stories with Susie and Jim, as well as on his own. He's grateful for his co-writers, family, and faith, buoying him during the pandemic of 2020-21, and this writing and publishing process.

CPSIA information can be obtained
at www.ICGtesting.com
Printed in the USA
LVHW012309190622
721628LV00004B/500

9 781954 023109